Sofia is on her way home by train from another boring business trip. A stranger approached her in the dark needing a bed for the night, she had the perfect place, an empty berth above her. He pleads his case, "I'm Chandler Riggs." He's broke and no place to sleep. With no time to think, her heart beating like a drum, she hesitates, but couldn't say no.

The next morning unexpectedly her life tumbles in turmoil when she walks up behind Chandler as he's telling the porter they are engaged to be married. What was he doing? She barely knew his name. She had to stop him, as she started a familiar voice echoed from behind her.

"Sofia! When were you going to tell me, you're getting married?" There he stood, the one man she could never lie to, her boss. Suddenly, she is faced with her dignity on the line, and again, no time to think, her heart beating like a drum, she hesitates, but said yes!

She is faced with the biggest decision of her life, tell the truth or see where it goes?

You had Me at Hello
Copyright © 2019 Riley Michaels
ISBN: 978-1-4874-2391-9
Cover art by Martine Jardin

Published by eXtasy Books Inc or
Devine Destinies, an imprint of eXtasy Books Inc

Look for us online at:
www.eXtasybooks.com or www.devinedestinies.com

You had Me at Hello

By

Riley Michaels

DEDICATION

To my husband with love!

CHAPTER ONE

Sofia Lincoln was returning home from another business trip. Had the decision been Sofia's, all business trips would have been removed from the menu. The train was pulling out from the passenger station, and she had one aisle to herself. For a while she sat and watched the countryside streaking past her. The mountains themselves seemed frozen in a geologic instant of upheaval. Monoliths of bare, thrusting granite, they rose harsh and unyielding and were, in a primeval way, beautiful. In places, time had softened their contours with a carpet of rich green forest but still hadn't conquered them. Exhausted from the craziness of the day, she was looking forward to a good night's rest. It would be a perfect ending to a long evening.

Sofia gently eased her hand into her purse, and, careful to not drop anything, she removed a pair of spongy ear plugs she kept just for special occasions. The plugs would help her sleep by dampening the loud noises from the bumping and jostling beneath her berth.

In nearly complete darkness, it was not easy to keep her footing on a moving train. Sofia stumbled around in her sleeping car, trying to be considerate and not wake anyone. Suddenly, out of the corner of her eye, she noticed someone standing in the middle of the aisle. Sofia shook her head slowly but didn't drop her gaze. Standing in the shadows, she peered into the darkness, straining for a better view of a tall, thin man, who was apparently walking towards her. Maybe he was a foreigner who couldn't speak English or was lost.

Had anyone seen this guy enter the compartment? Sofia's heart raced with fear, and, shaking in her shoes, she stepped closer to get a better look at the stranger. Sofia eyed the handsome man warily, strongly aware of his presence. It unsettled her to be fixated on a man she couldn't clearly see.

He was easily more than six feet tall, with broad shoulders and slim hips. The black suit adorning him was tailored to his body in a way that left nothing to her imagination, and he wore it with the ease of a man clearly accustomed to the finer things in life. His face was classically handsome, high cheek bones contrasting with bright-blue eyes with an expression of intelligence. There was a smile on a strong mouth, a mouth every woman would like to stick their lips to, including Sofia. He had a confident smile and an eager expression.

He was a perfect stranger, and chances were there would never again be another moment like this. Her amused curiosity turned to dismay when she realized he was approaching her. Sure enough, he stopped right in front of her, pulled out a boarding pass, and held it in his hand.

What can he possibly want from me?

A kind of stillness hung in the air. Nothing happened and nothing was said.

Sofia wasn't a stranger to one-night stands. He was attractive enough for her to sleep with. There was nothing written anywhere that stated she must be married to have sex with a man. Strength and passion seized her, and she did like her fun. Sensible as she was, she never kept a man long enough to settle down with him.

"I'm sorry if I startled you, ma'am," he said in a loud whisper, obviously taking care not to wake anyone. "Please allow me to introduce myself. I'm Chandler Riggs. I am hoping you will let me stay with you tonight." His voice sounded oddly reasonable.

Had he said what Sofia thought she'd heard? Be that as it might, chances like this never happened to her. Her first impulse was to blurt out *no*, then yell for the porter, yet the words never made it to her lips. Satisfying her curiosity, she allowed her gaze to roam freely over him. He was magnificently made. This guy had her all right—right in the palm of his hand.

Her eyes widened, lips parted from a touch of panic, and a sense of sudden awareness came, but he was just a man, a perfect specimen of the male species, but still a man.

With a sigh of relief and a bit of effort, Sofia concluded she was unable to articulate any questions, even in her mind. It was her last night away in the middle of nowhere. Who would know if she had her fun? "Please," she started in a quivery voice, lifting a hand to indicate her reluctance to move forward. "Are there no other sleeping berths available?" she managed to say without difficulty.

"Of course," he conceded. "Unfortunately, I am not able to pay for one." He hesitated, breaking eye contact. "To be honest, if I may, I lost all my money at the casino in Monte Carlo. Please, you mustn't think I'm a compulsive gambler. That was my first time, and my last. It was a very expensive lesson," Chandler exclaimed quietly.

She gritted her teeth and smiled. "This train left from Nice, not Monte Carlo," she parried quickly. It was a lie, and she knew it. That was easy enough, or so she thought.

"Don't I know, ma'am. I was able to obtain a ticket." Chandler looked at her steadily. "I had to hitch a ride in Monte Carlo, and I walked a good part of the way. While in Nice, I looked for someone who would take pity and lend me enough money for a ticket. All I could manage to borrow was enough for a one-way ticket to Paris. I'd be very grateful if you were to let me use your empty berth just for tonight," he said. "I can pay you for the price of a ticket when we get there. I would truly be grateful."

He seemed like the type who was used to getting what he wanted. Instead being turned off, Sofia found him even more interesting. A man with no scruples and way too much ambition. "Where's your luggage?"

"I couldn't pay my hotel bill either, so they kept my things until I can get back to pick them up. As you can see, I'm in a rather difficult position. Once I get to Paris, I'll be all right. I have friends waiting for me there." His impromptu explanation sounded reasonable.

"Why didn't you get in touch with your friends in Paris before boarding the train?" Sofia inquired softly. "They could have sent you the money for a berth."

He turned to face her. "There wasn't time. I have a very important meeting in Paris," he snapped. "Look, I know all this must seem strange to you, but it is true, I assure you. If my situation doesn't inspire you to take pity, then I'll leave and ask you to please accept my sincere apologies. Besides, you don't seem to be the type of person who could be so cruel."

Thinking of her own exhaustion and happy to have the berth, she decided it would be cruel to deny as good looking a man as Chandler a good night's sleep. She studied his lean, good-humored face, considering his honesty. "My intuition tells me I'll be safe with you. You don't look the least bit dangerous," she responded. "I don't make a habit of doing such things as this, as long as you know." Being forced to sit up through the entire trip would have been grueling. "Are you sure sleeping is all you want?"

Hesitant, with eyes half-mast, her handsome stranger's calmness made Sofia's heart pound. How stupid was she to have asked that? She'd made a fool of herself without letting anyone else in on it.

"I can assure you, madame, I've no intention of harming you nor anyone. I wouldn't have intruded on you otherwise. I'll be asleep in no time." For a moment, a strange feeling of uncontrollable fire was flooding through his veins. His mind was clear—Sofia was the woman he had been searching for to share his life. His face glowed with pleasure and relief as he put one hand on the upper berth and lifted himself in.

She was standing there so innocently. *Doesn't she know what she does to a man? Can't she ever guess?* Just because he had given his word that the berth was all he wanted, it didn't mean he wasn't affected by the sight of her—in the dark—that left everything to the imagination.

Loaning her berth may have been Sofia's undoing.

In the berth beneath Chandler lay a beautiful woman, long slender legs and a set of warm lips just waiting to be seized. His mind tumbled over itself in its frenzy. It wasn't that he didn't want to say anything, because he did. He was confident of himself and his future.

Sofia had a final word of caution. "I'm sure you know how strict the railway is with these things. If one of the attendants should discover you are here without a ticket—"

Chandler merely whispered lightly, "You can turn the light out if you like. Sleep well."

On a train in the middle of nowhere, who'd know if she had sex with a gorgeous stranger? Sofia cared, but then she didn't care. She lay quiet and heard her stranger thrashing around, maybe removing his coat and shoes. Sofia wanted to join her handsome stranger.

There was no getting around it—Sofia wanted him. And what she wanted, she usually got. Who would ever know if she pursued her desire to sleep with a man she'd just met?

Even though the curtains were drawn all night, Sofia was unable to break free of her desire for the stranger in her berth. There was something different about this guy—she could feel it to the bone. Lying quietly in the dark, it seemed like it was long into the night before Sofia finally gave way to a restless sleep. But she thought mostly about the man named Chandler Riggs, who was lying in the berth above her head.

Strange as the situation was, she pushed the blankets away in the darkness and lay still, feeling her heart beat more wildly than ever. Within the confines of her mind, no words were needed. Visualizing her handsome stranger, she caught her breath sharply, the warmth of flames moving up her legs to meet in a soaring blaze beyond her. His lips, warm and moist against hers, him easing his tongue in for a touch of hers. Him releasing the tenderness of her lips to blaze a warm trail to her breasts. With a featherlight touch, he caressed one breast then captured the other as he nipped at her tiny hard nipple with his teeth, teasing beyond her self-control.

She clawed fiercely, imagining digging her nails into his back as he wasted no time reaching his destination. He separated her legs with a long, slow glide, tantalizing her, knowing before suddenly overtaking her swelling desire, gently tightening his lips to suck easily, tightly and easy again, over and over until her control was no more. She couldn't hold back any longer as he brought her to orgasm. When she returned to her body, she was limp and breathless, listening to the soft ringing in her ears. She was barely conscious. For a moment she hardly knew he was above her. It seemed a strange thing to her that a time of such intimate closeness had passed so easily. The moment of great ecstasy was experienced alone, as fleeting as a puff of air.

"Whoa," she murmured once the sensation was over,

leaving her giddy and lightheaded.

It was daybreak. Within seconds Sofia was reveling in the sensation of golden rays against her skin. She stirred in half-awakened ecstasy and stretched, then rolled over, snuggling deeper in the downy berth as she hugged a pillow to her. She inhaled deeply and released her breath with a grateful sigh. She opened her eyes, then sat up with a start. Her awareness of the occupied berth above her sent her thoughts racing with a fleetness that only intrigue could provoke.

The light glaring through the curtains fell on an unusually dark spot on the sheets. Could she have spilled something on her outfit and didn't realize it? Could it be something she rubbed against and didn't see? Sofia was wearing the same outfit as the day before and in one quick thought, she figured it out. "Oh, no." Panic-stricken, she knew exactly where the spot came from. "You've got to be fucking kidding me," she whispered to herself. "I can't believe this is happening. I'll just ignore it and pass it off as something I spilled if anyone mentions it." That was her story and she was sticking to it.

Having read this from the pages of magazines, she knew it was possible to experience an orgasm in a dream, and for herself, Sofia wanted more.

Surely, no one would say anything about it. They knew people took food to their berths and spilling happened—it was a bumpy ride. The more she thought about that reason, the better it sounded. How could she have put herself in such a precarious position? She was letting her imagination get away with her.

Restless, Sofia reached for her handbag. There was an item she always carried. She opened the bag and reached inside to retrieve an ivory-handled hairbrush her mother had loaned her. Looking at it brought back memories of times as a child when her grandmother would brush her hair at bedtime and tell stories of how things were when she was Sofia's age.

Slowly, Sofia brushed her long, soft locks, stroke by stroke, her head tilted sideways. Her hair was beautiful when left long and flowing. The brush was the only possession her grandmother had passed down to Sofia's mother, and would one day be hers. All was quiet with her secret sleeper—not even as much as a snore.

There was no longer the bright, warm sunlight of the Riviera. The day was turning cloudy and looked like rain might pour any minute. Marseilles was well behind them, but she couldn't be sure if they had passed Lyons.

Maybe she should offer breakfast together. He had no money. Had he thought about eating? He must be hungry. For some reason Sofia had the urge to check her bag to make sure nothing had been taken. Only opening the top, she could see everything without having to disturb anything. All was in the same place. Her effects included an antique gold pillbox given to her from an aunt. Her aunt had since passed, but the pillbox was worth more in sentimental value than in dollars. Sofia glanced up. Each berth had its own clock, and for one reason or another she kept looking at that clock.

A wash and freshening up would be the thing, since Sofia had spent the night in her street clothes. It appeared she wasn't the only one thinking the same way. Would there be any hot water left? It would hold her until she got home to her own.

It was an elegant washroom, a cozy one-person corner not much smaller than her closet at home, but there was one small detail she had overlooked—the washroom was for every berth in the compartment.

Feeling slightly embarrassed, Sofia climbed out of bed

and looked in the upper berth to see if he was still there and hadn't died on her sometime in the night. Yep, her handsome stranger was still there, facing towards the window, sound asleep. Disturbing him was out—he needed his sleep, and chances were he'd be gone by time she returned from freshening up.

Was she being silly or horny? Why would she be worrying about what this guy thought of her? She'd never worried about that before. The only thing that was different in this case was she wanted him and aimed to have him. *He just needs to make the first move.*

With her mind set, if Chandler did make the first move, she wasn't going to pull away. Sleeping with a man you just met really wasn't uncommon for her generation. Many singles were opting for the single life with no strings. On the other hand, it would give her handsome stranger a chance to freshen up for breakfast and join her. The time was now eight AM, and breakfast was being served in the dining car. Sofia decided to go and leave her handsome stranger asleep in his berth, unable to get him off her mind. If he was gone when she returned, at least she had done a good deed and helped someone out of a bind

In the light of day, the aisle was crowded with people who had been sitting up all night. After seeing there wasn't enough room to cuss a cat, in the company of scads of noisy, pushy tourists, Sofia decided to pass on breakfast. She wasn't that hungry anyway.

The train was on schedule to reach Paris within the hour and pull into the Gare de Lyon Station, where she could leisurely enjoy a cup of coffee, and maybe a snack. It would be nice if her handsome stranger would join her. The thought of him being hungry crossed her mind. Could he afford breakfast? Had he even eaten dinner the night before? She would offer to buy him a meal. She'd given him a place to sleep for the night. What would be wrong with a meal? He seemed to be a proud man, though, and might turn the offer down.

"I'm being ridiculous," Sofia said to herself. "I'm not letting this go any further—he is driving me crazy, and I don't even know him." But she wanted to go further. She wanted to have sex with him. She lingered in the passageway of the dining car, waiting until the very last minute to return to the man in her berth, the opposite of Jasper, her previous lover. Jasper was brown-haired, short, and smiled very little. He took life very seriously, something her stranger didn't seem to do, and it was attractive. She was beginning to realize a little more imagination could make life a lot more interesting.

Standing in the doorway, blocking the entrance of her compartment, Chandler was engaged in a heated discussion with the attendant, and neither noticed her. Sofia decided to go back to her berth. When she heard what Chandler was saying, she could barely believe a single word of what she was hearing. The longer she stood in silence the more surprising the conversation become.

"But, my dear man, I've just finished telling you! We had a silly argument and went our separate ways. It's not unusual for such things to happen with newlyweds. Just to show my wife, I took a first-class ticket, so I wouldn't have to travel with her. When I saw the berth was free, I came in to make my peace. I hope you're not going to hold it against me because I came to talk to my wife."

"But this passenger is listed under the name of Mademoiselle Lincoln."

"Just a slip. Understandable, isn't it, considering we've only been married for two days?" He looked up, to see Sofia. "Isn't that right, darling? Tell this man your name is Madame Riggs and I am your husband."

With her mouth slightly agape, she looked at the porter, and for some reason she nodded *yes*.

Having recovered from the initial shock, Sofia found the whole thing amusing. He had no money, and he was drop-dead gorgeous. Now she had him by the balls and he knew it. She had never been put on the spot like this before and found it funny. She could hardly abandon him now. After all, he was her husband. For how long was yet to be determined.

To save Chandler from being questioned by the police as a stowaway—it could mean trouble for him if caught—she couldn't see any harm in playing along. Besides, he had an important meeting in Paris, and one word from her would make everything so much simpler.

"Of course," she said happily, "he's my husband." She smiled. Now the smirk was on her face.

Gratitude immediately shone in Chandler's eyes.

"Sofia, is it possible? Are you married?" She knew that voice from behind her. "Oh, no," she whispered quietly. Now *she* was in a pickle and needed Chandler to cover for *her*.

Sofia spun around to come face-to-face with her boss. A simple persuasion had now just turned into something more serious. What had she done? All for the sake of a roll in the hay that had yet to happen. Poised, his voice ringing through her ears, she cast a sweeping glance over his head. What she was looking for, even she didn't know. Just for the moment it seemed as if an old love's shadow passed by. Within a split second the vision left her.

Sofia could keep outward appearances normal. "Monsieur Parlay! What are you doing here?" Stepping back from his hard gaze, Sofia drew a deep breath, so nervous she could hardly speak.

"I boarded at Marseilles, dear. I had some business to attend to at our branch office there. I just heard the news, marvelous news." His face was glowing so bright, you'd think he was the one who got married. Mr. Parlay was well known by the attendants on the train, so there were no further questions from the staff, who hurried away as the train approached its next stop.

"It certainly happened quick. Love at first sight, maybe, one could say? You youngsters today, nothing like it was when I was your age. We're blocking the passageway here, let's step inside and you can introduce me to the lucky fellow," Parlay urged them eagerly. He seemed beside himself, wanting to hear all about it.

Much to her alarm, her moments of freedom as she knew it slid by her with frightening speed.

"We don't have the time right now to go into the details," Parlay spoke up. "My chauffeur will be waiting to pick me up. Why don't I give you both a ride home? That way you won't have to worry about finding a taxi, and you can tell me all about everything on the way. Two lovebirds! Wait for me here. I must go and get my attaché case from the luggage department."

Dumbfounded, Sofia and Chandler stood staring at one another. There was a twinkle of amusement in Chandler's eyes, but Sofia was in an absolute panic. Something cold gripped her, sending a shivery spasm through her body.

"What in the hell did you do?" Sofia angrily blurted. "I don't know you, and you sure as hell don't know me!"

"Me? What did I do? I've never met the man in my life."

"Yeah, you! I don't know you, I don't know anything about you, and now look! How clear does it have to be? I know you're not stupid, are you?" Drawing a deep breath for a second time, she blurted out, "I can't believe this is happening to me, of all things. You should be ashamed of yourself, ashamed." She was so angry that she could have thrown him from the train in the middle of nowhere.

"Who is this man you're in such a tizzy over?" Chandler

whispered, with both brows raised.

"Oh my God, Monsieur Parlay is my boss. He's a charming man, quite marvelous really, but this is one time in my life when I'm anything but happy to see him!" She spoke in a loud whisper. "Of all people to run into on a train, why couldn't it have been anyone but him. Him!" She threw up her hands.

Chandler gently patted her shoulder. "Now don't panic, everything will work its way out, just you wait and see."

"*Just you wait and see.*" Sofia shook her head in disgust. "It had better, for your sake. Damn it!" She was angry, and the longer she stood thinking about it, the more upset she got. "Just follow my lead and don't stray. If you do, he'll know, and I'll have to kill you."

"It will be okay, I promise," Chandler smiled.

"I'll be okay," she mimicked him a second time. "Shut up, you've caused enough damage already, and I don't even know you."

Parlay walked into the compartment and touched Sofia by the arm. "Come, my dear, the limo is over there. Your luggage was on the platform, and my chauffeur loaded it and is waiting for us. You only have the one suitcase between the two of you? Well, of course, it's much more convenient to have your luggage sent directly to your home . . .but I didn't."

In the general confusion of pushing and shoving, it was impossible to speak at a normal level. Once they were in the limo, things weren't the same. Parlay made Chandler sit up front next to the chauffeur, while he and Sofia sat in the back. The limo wasn't equipped with a glass partition between the front and back seats, making it easier for Chandler to turn. His expression was a mixture of confusion, mystery—and a certain amount of glee.

"I must say your marriage has come as quite a surprise,

Sofia," Parlay began. "It doesn't seem like you to act so hastily without saying a word to anyone—"

What had Parlay been about to say? To mention Jasper, perhaps? Behind the door, no one knew what Jasper was really like, and Sofia was tired of him handling her any way that suited him. The abuse was over. She knew this wasn't the time to say anything about him—it was never a good time to mention Jasper. She hated him for the way he treated her.

Parlay went on, "How did you meet? I mean, you haven't said a word about him."

"Oh, by chance," mumbled Sofia, feeling the dishonesty rising and embarrassed to say anything about the truth for fear of harm to her reputation. What was she to do? What was she to say?

"Of, course! You were with Amanda. She knows people wherever she goes. Didn't she come back with you? Oh, what am I saying, of course not! She'd want to leave the two of you to have a romantic train ride."

Sofia knew she would need to straighten out this business of her alleged husband, but she couldn't think of how to go about doing it. Parlay was very traditional, and she enjoyed working for him and hoped to move up in the ranks of the company one day. What she would find amusing, despite her initial wariness, he would see as tasteless. Of that she had no doubt. Sofia jumped at the opportunity to talk about Amanda.

As soon as Chandler was out of sight, she'd explain the entire situation to Parlay and beg for an effort toward forgiveness for making up this story. Having Chandler there didn't help matters, either. He would be embarrassed, Sofia assumed. He was handsome, gentle, and lovable, with his dark curls and bright blue eyes that nearly glowed in the dark. She had hoped once they reached her building, he would find a reason to leave. If not, she'd send him to the store for something.

You won't believe this, Mr. Riggs isn't really my husband . . . She would tell the truth as simply as possible. Then she could resume the quiet, normal life she had known before — a life without intrigue or adventure. Oh, yes it would be great to have such things out of her life. She had learned her lesson, yet she couldn't apologize for wanting this handsome stranger in her bed. Parlay needn't know about any of that! Luckily, Sofia had a way about her, and she usually got what she wanted and often more than expected.

She managed to keep her secret—she was all woman, and a woman with desires for the company of the opposite sex. Sofia lived her life like a wild bird, trusting her instincts and following the pull of her heart, contrary to all reason and logic. The instinct was to spread her wings and fly. But since she'd never tasted real freedom, she could identify the restless longing for what it was.

With her softly curving body, strongly defined face and faintly amused tilt of her chin, she seemed to think of herself as unattractive, like the ugly duckling in the classic tale, but she was a swan—every bit as lovely, every bit as regal.

The inner reflections were as multifaceted as a diamond, their brilliance burning twice as bright. Chandler had recognized it—he could see it in her eyes, beyond her smile and outward calm.

The limo had left Boulevard Saint-German and was traveling up Rue De Sevres toward her place on Rue Vanneau.

The sky was cloudless, except for a grayish haze hanging over the city. Against the racing clouds, tall chimneys and the cracked and broken chimney pots squeezed their way through lightly. It would be another suffocating day in Paris. Those who were forced to stay in the city would be taking advantage of the early morning breeze. While children played in the street, women were chatting in front of open doorways, and Sofia's concierge was sitting in her chair, dozing.

Every one of Sofia's acquaintances knew Ireland Taxon. She was a large woman in her early fifties whose effusive chatter masked a heart of gold. Ireland had been taking care of the nine-story building for thirty-five years and considered herself the official overseer of everything. When Ireland wasn't scolding her tenants for ridiculous things that weren't any of her business, she was showering her tenants with motherly love. She considered the tenants her children and often told Sofia she was her favorite—*a beautiful girl, she really needs someone at night.*

When Sofia saw Ireland in her chair, she began to worry. *Lord, please get me through this.* Just as she thought that, Parlay jumped out of the limo and shouted from the top of his lungs, announcing he was delivering a pair of newlyweds. Sofia would have been just as happy if the Ireland hadn't taken it upon herself to look after her.

Ireland looked shocked, but she bounced out of her chair as quickly as her weight would allow, shrieking with joy. "My God! Monsieur Parlay, did I hear you right?"

"Well, of course . . . Mademoiselle Sofia and this gorgeous young man! What a happy moment. All the best to you, dear, and your husband. Welcome home!"

Ireland was beside herself, squeezing cheeks and gloating over the newlyweds.

With an enchanting look, Chandler thanked Ireland.

"Well, I must say, you've caught a handsome one, Sofia." Ireland laughed out loud. "And not only that, he's distinguished, too. I know a sophisticated man when I see one.

The two of you will bring the entire building good luck. Except for Mademoiselle Sofia, all my tenants are either widowed or old married couples. Now, there will be new life in this dreary old building. We'll feel young again. No, no. Don't let the chauffeur take the suitcase up. Anyway, I have the keys to the apartment, and no one could get in without me. Allow me, Monsieur Chandler. I've carried heavier in my time, believe me. You just look after your wife. Come along and I'll take you on a tour."

Sofia had never seen Ireland like this. One would have thought she was the one who got married. She wasn't hurting anyone, and Sofia didn't want to rain on her parade, so she let her go without a word of ridicule.

CHAPTER TWO

Sofia helplessly witnessed the whole scene. She might as well forget about sending Chandler away now. If she so much as suggested he go to the store, Ireland surely would insist on accompanying him. What would be the point in sending him away? She was beginning to feel dizzy. Now was the perfect time for the play time she wanted, and to get away with it easily.

What was she to do? Why were these people so happy to see her married? And why didn't Chandler ever speak up to stop her? A few words from him would have cleared up the whole affair. Instead, he was dispensing charm and relishing in all the fuss.

"Well, I can see that I'm leaving you in good hands, Sofia," said Parlay. "And don't worry about the office. Take tomorrow off—in fact, take the entire week. You and Chandler need a little time to get settled in. I won't expect you until next Monday, and not a day sooner."

Sofia cringed at the word *husband* but said goodbye to her boss and thanked him. Chandler and Parlay shook hands, Ireland picked up the suitcase, and away they went. None of this would have ever happened had Chandler not needed a damn berth to sleep in.

What had started out as a joke quickly turned to reality. She was ready to strangle Chandler for what he'd done. There was one good thing to come out of this—she had her man and needed no excuse to explain when he came and went. What kind of a pickle had Sofia found herself in?

She'd covered for Chandler and turned around to have him cover for her.

Sofia thought hard about this. Yes, that was what she would say. By this time, she was becoming desperate. She couldn't get him off her mind, since things like this don't happen to her. It was nice, and he was worth pursuing. The only real thing on Sofia's mind was ripping the clothes from Chandler's body, revealing his bare skin for her nurturing. The moment and timing couldn't have been better. Who'd know any different? She didn't know she was married till this morning. When she was done with him, all she would have to say was that he left her for another woman.

On the threshold, Chandler stopped for a second and asked Sofia what she wanted him to do.

Seeing a blank expression on his face, and overcome by the events of the past ten minutes, Sofia merely motioned for him what she wanted him to do.

If only Parlay hadn't been on the train! If only everything hadn't gone wrong—all wrong. Sofia was caught in a chain of circumstances she had no control over, and there didn't seem to be any end to it. Chandler—look at what he had done to her! What was worse, Sofia had gone along, right along with his devious plan. He, who was the cause of this incredible mess, was smiling, and Sofia could have slapped the smile right off his quirky expression.

"I knew you'd be coming in on the fifteenth, Mademoiselle Sofia. So, yesterday, I let myself into your apartment and tidied it up a bit. It was a good thing. Someone sent you flowers this morning," Ireland commented, with an air of excitement in her tone. The elevator took an eternity to come. Ireland, cursing, slammed the palm of her hand futilely against the lighted arrow pointing upward and seemed to consider taking the stairs. At last, the elevator arrived.

"What the hell, Ireland! I don't need you cleaning my

place up." Sofia hesitated. "I have asked you how many times to stay out of my apartment. If you do it again, I'm looking for another place to live." Sofia had wanted so bad to say that to Ireland, nose to nose. Only Sofia didn't want to show her bad side, and how it was beginning to form within her mind.

They left the elevator on the third floor. With her usual briskness, using her free arm, Ireland reached for the lock and opened the door to Sofia's apartment, then marched right in as if she lived there. Not that she didn't own the building. Sofia was infuriated as Ireland opened the door for her.

Sophia wondered what Chandler would think of her space. The living room was large, one wall made entirely of glass, with a balcony beyond overlooking the streets below. The walls were vanilla, the floors parqueted in exotic light woods. The painting, carvings and furniture were contemporary and so abstract in design that Sofia had never been sure which chunk of carved brazilwood was meant for sitting. She finally opted for the cheaper sofa, but as soon as she'd sat down she figured out it was a poor choice. The piece of furniture seemed to be wrapping itself insolently around her derriere, almost forcing her into a reclining position.

She peered inside the large, comfortable bedroom and took a quick peek into the walk-in-closet and the en suite bath. The furnishings were much more traditional than those in the living-room—the rosewood bed, burau and writing table were immediately recognizable by Chandler. Except for the abstract oil paintings, whose subject matter he recognized right off. A huge spotted palm occupied one entire corner of the bedroom, and the bedspread and drapes were of a crisp batik in vibrant greens and yellows, so that there was a primitive aura of the jungle in the room that somehow managed to put Sofia at ease.

"You must excuse the furnishings," Sofia told Chandler, crossing the room to put as much distance as she could betweenher and Ireland before she said something she'd regret.

"As you can see, Monsieur Riggs, this is a lovely apartment," Ireland commented, turning to Chandler staring, "Mademoiselle Sofia takes very good care of it . . .and she has such good taste. Look at the entranceway, it's like a miniature gallery, wouldn't you say? To the left, here's the bathroom, and the kitchen to your right."

Ireland was bustling around the apartment opening shutters, rearranging things, all the while putting on the charm with the apartment as a coverup for her intentions.

"As you may have noticed, the place reflects the predilections of its owner," Ireland commented. "You'll find everything very comfortable here. We have all the conveniences. It's a real gem, this place is."

"Ireland, may I have a moment with you? I must say something.," Sofia said.

"Certainly," Ireland replied, looking curious and every bit the great landlady.

"Have I ever been late on my rent?" Sofia regarded Ireland with confusion.

"Oh, heavens no. Why would I ever be concerned with such a thing?" Ireland stood staring at Sofia.

"Well, I don't mean to be a booger, but stay out of my apartment unless I ask you to help, or I'm behind in my rent. Don't do it again, okay? I don't know how much plainer I can be, Ireland. I don't want anyone in my apartment when I'm away, okay?"

"I suppose," Ireland replied with a metallic hiss—the sound Sofia supposed a serpent would make if it could speak.

"I'll see you tomorrow, Ireland . . . tomorrow!" Sofia urged, although it seemed Ireland's jaw tightened a little. Despite whatever admirable qualities Ireland might have possessed, she was still nosey and invasive.

"Very well." She hesitated, then turned sharply, and looked up at the ceiling as if she had seen a bug or something crawling around.

"Think about it," Sofia snapped. "Stop! This apartment I pay for, I don't need anyone running around changing the way I like my furniture, opening my windows, cleaning, and whatever else. I like for my things to be in the same spot when I'm here and when I'm gone. You are coming in and out at your convenience. What a mess this is, and it's getting worse as we speak!" Sofia screamed. "Ireland, you have no right to be in my apartment without my knowledge, and if I catch you doing this again without me asking, I will move and let you rent this place to someone that won't pay their rent."

Ireland continued her chatter.

Sofia could have said anything—reland wasn't paying any mind to her.

"Here are your flowers . . .I'm sure Monsieur Riggs will want to use that little room as a study. Having a husband is much better than sharing the apartment with a stranger."

Sofia tried to ignore that churning feeling in the pit of her stomach. "I'll change the locks if I must. I'm not interested in what you think, Ireland. I've lived here five years, and not one time have I ever been late with my rent," Sofia demanded angrily. She was on the verge of kicking Ireland out.

After a moment, Sofia decided, "That's it, I'm changing my lock tomorrow. I'll keep that bat out one way or another."

Completely overcome, Sofia made herself comfortable sitting on the sofa, her face buried in her hands, weeping bitterly. Sofia was in much better humor when Ireland left her apartment.

Chandler stepped out with Ireland on her way to the elevator. "You are very wise, Madame Ireland," he said calmly, "and you have been very kind. I'm sure we'll be happy here and I'm certainly happy to have met you. We'll see you later, and thank you again for all you have done." When he returned, the roles were reversed—it was a concerned Chandler who turned to face Sofia. "Sofia!" he urged, distress obvious in his voice, as he quickly crossed the room to put the palm of his hand gently on her shoulder.

"All that old bat needs is one about a foot long put to her and she'll shut up a while and give me some peace," Sofia spouted off in anger. Ireland had been bad before, but this was over the line, and Sofia was at the end of her wits.

"Sofia!" Chandler bit back quickly. "You are intent on going about this, aren't you?"

"I don't mean to displease you," she said uneasily. "Oh, I don't want your sympathy, I meant what I said," she replied, hopelessly furious, lifting her head. "If it weren't for you, I wouldn't be in this awful mess. And Jasper—"

"Who is Jasper? Your real husband?"

"No . . . no," she answered quietly, feeling the blood drain from her face. Conversation, though hushed, held an element of anticipation as Sofia and Chandler were alone, finally.

"Your fiancé?"

"Not yet . . . he was going to be at one time, but it's over and has been for a little while." Suddenly bewildered, she added, "Besides, why are you interested?"

"Do you still love him?" Chandler gazed at her for a moment, his face void of any expression, then suddenly the scowl reappeared.

"Of course! Well, I mean . . . oh, no, I don't know . . . . relationships aren't really for me. I'm the single type," Sofia stuttered as she paced back and forth nervously.

"If you love him, my coming into your life may have stopped you from doing something you would regret. You should thank me, from the sounds of it."

"*Thank* you!" she shouted indignantly. "Thank you? After all you've done?" Her mouth felt dry and her heart continued to pound against her chest in anger. Sofia kept wondering why he stayed so positive all the time.

"Why should I feel guilty, any more than you?" he asked. "Before we start our first argument, I think we'd better have something to eat. I'm starving, and I know you must be."

Sofia quieted down and looked at him. Who was this guy? What was this guy? This was getting stranger by the minute. "I've been away for a little while, so I doubt if there's anything more than a few dried-out cookies in the place." She turned to him, a flutter of pleasure rippling through her.

"Forget the cookies. You aren't in any shape to go out. I can find a store to get supper . . . if you don't mind me doing so," Chandler countered.

"No, I'm good with it. Let me get you some money." Sofia rummaged through her purse to find a few francs hidden in the bottom lining. "Here, get what you like. You couldn't do more harm than what's already been done."

Chandler had an easy way with people. His gaze swept back to her with great intensity, with his heart coming to a standstill. He had known the companionship of beautiful women in the most sophisticated cities of the world. He could not believe he had found the most beautiful one of them all.

Chandler could hardly bear the agony of the thought of not seeing her again. He made no effort to move or leave.

His throat tightened, his mind overflowing with her face, her body, the delightful way tiny dimples appeared at the corners of her mouth when she smiled.

But the fact was undeniable. Chandler wanted to make love to her. He wanted to take her immediately, and he didn't want to keep himself in restraint another moment. How much more could he endure without throwing her down and satisfying himself with her?

Yet he couldn't let himself make love to her, no matter how much he wanted. She was a woman, and all women were alike. She could be forced from his mind. He'd never known one who couldn't. If she were homely, it could be possible to push her from his mind. But how could he? Sofia was so beautiful, completely desirable and now—so close at hand.

But Sofia was different, and it wasn't fair for him to say that she wasn't. The others had all been willing and eager partners in the games of love. Sofia was innocent.

"I have been cruel to take you from the pleasant life. You were happy, and I should be damned for forcing you from it." He paused, his face grim and his mouth drawn downward at the corners. It was a great heaviness upon his chest that he truly felt bad for.

"It's not enough that everybody now thinks that you are my husband," Sofia muttered in exasperation, "but on top of everything else, you happen to be broke." She hesitated. "Like the story of my life," she whispered. Sofia wondered whether it was his engaging, easygoing manner or perhaps some inner facet of his personality that was responsible for his charm. It didn't make it easy to know that he was right.

With a strangled cry, she felt the color burning deeper into her face and wanted to hate him to the bone.

He took the money without displaying the slightest sign of embarrassment. "Thank you. You mustn't think I just go around having my way paid by young women." He had resumed his lighthearted tone, apparently concerned.

"You could pay me back in the old-fashioned way." Sofia smiled with no regard. *I'll never see him again. A ten-franc note is like money from heaven to a man like him.* She was finding it difficult to know what to think about this guy. *Oh, to hell with him! He's made a fool out of me right in front of my boss, friends and Lord only knows who else that might have seen us together!* She gritted her teeth in frustration. *Men like him only think of themselves and the hell with others.*

He was in her life one minute and out the next. Just like that—walk in, walk out, no appointment necessary. Sofia was hungry, and there was still no sign of Chandler. She felt bad about what she'd said, but if he didn't come back maybe it would be for the best. All she was attracted to was his features—the man she had dreamed of her whole life. She needed to summon previously unknown reserves of self-control.

There was something pleasant about the situation. Now, after about 45 minutes, Sofia was beginning to think she was right about having given him the money. *Has he run off? It's starting to look that way.* Having such a handsome man around certainly added a little spice to her life. She couldn't deny that, and perhaps it explained the sudden surge of joy she'd felt when he was in front of her, someone she could reach out and touch.

About an hour passed, and the doorbell rang like a wild animal. Sofia ran quickly to the door. "Hold on, I'm right here . . . . Hold on!" she yelled out loudly a second time. It was Chandler, his arms loaded with bags of groceries, leaning on the doorbell.

After staring at him for a long second, she shouted her surprise. "You're back! What on earth have you done?

Where did you get all this food? I didn't give you enough money. Get in here."

"I have things that would satisfy the most ferocious appetite—eggs, ham, milk, cheese, and java. Let's get to the kitchen, and don't you worry about it," he said as he struggled with the groceries. Chandler reached into his pocket to retrieve Sofia's change. "Here's your change back—one franc, twenty centimes." Chandler smiled. "I want you to know that I'm not a bad guy. I would never take money that doesn't belong to me."

The change might come in handy if he needed to take the train for one reason or another. She gestured vaguely and left the change laying on the counter.

"Doesn't matter," Sofia said, grateful for the food, and the fact that he'd come back to her with his arms full. What was she to think of him now, or could this be a scam? She didn't have anything of real value anyone would want to scam her for. So why think it?

"You're an angel. An angel in a very bad mood, mind you, but an angel just the same."

"And contrary to what you may think, I am very scrupulous about paying my debts. That might explain how I get in and out of debt so often," Sofia added.

"Oh, I must warn you. When I went out for food, something happened that you may not like." Chandler hesitated. "I think you might need to know your nice neighbor Madame Taxon was trying to find out what I was doing and insisted on going with me to the store, then introduced me everywhere we went as your husband." He smirked—at least, at first. Chandler's expression didn't change as Sofia looked at him intently.

"Ugh," Sofia groaned. She met his gaze and raised a mocking eyebrow but didn't smile, and knew he was just being himself, whatever that might be. "Oh, that freaking woman could aggravate the horns of a Billy-goat," she whispered. While she talked, she was busily unwrapping everything.

Things have gone too far. Going over what had happened on the train, Sofia felt Chandler's last few words hit her like a brick. He had been introduced everywhere as her husband. "As my husband," she screeched. How would she ever be able to explain the whole thing had been nothing but a lie? With a sigh, she leaned against the counter. "All this over one night's sleep in an empty berth," she whispered under her breath.

Sofia's back began to ache, and she leaned her head on the door. She closed her eyes, but they fluttered with nervousness. Her stomach gnawed at her. Finally, she straightened and stared at Chandler.

He met her gaze.

She continued staring, as if he could read her thoughts from across the room. It was hard to know what to really make of him after last night. There were obviously more layers to him than she had first suspected. She was willing to admit she might have imagined his sinister smile.

"What's the matter?" Chandler asked. "Are you tired or something? Or did I supposedly wear you out last night?"

"You have all the nerve!" she replied indignantly. "We didn't do anything last night." Sofia thought hard, but her abysmal lack of imagination defeated her.

"What I meant was, you haven't taken your coat off since we got home. Look . . . why don't you lie down and rest for a few minutes? Give me your hand." Chandler smiled.

Sofia was hesitant, but he reached for it anyway.

Chandler smiled. "Your hand," he repeated, taking hold as if it were his own. With his head bent, he examined her fingers, tracing each one with an unhurried fingertip.

His touch was featherlight, yet Sofia felt as if every cell of her skin were coming alive. "What are you doing?" she rasped.

"What am I doing? I know how to look at a woman and tell what kind of love will bring a sparkle to her eyes, warm her skin tone, and make her feel more beautiful than ever."

Sofia felt dumbfounded, with a captive hand. "You can tell all that just by looking at a woman?"

The glance he gave her was tinged with irony. "I must talk to her as well, but of course, you and I have already been talking." Chandler took his time and didn't let go of her hand. "Your fingers are long and slender. You would wear a beautiful marquise cut. For your fair skin, a diamond in a simple silver setting, and because you're tall, the stone should be no smaller than two carats."

Sofia looked up at Chandler. His face seemed to radiate with pride. She pulled her hand away and gave him a coy smile. "It seems that you're great at a lot of things." For a moment she said nothing more, then suddenly added, "Stay away from the trash can. It's full and I missed the garbage pick-up." The silence was acute—*where did that come from*? How stupid of her.

Chandler stared at her a moment, then drew his head back and laughed heartily. "Now, don't you go and put a damper on our first week of marriage. We had a lovely honeymoon and now we're back." He smiled happily.

"We *what*? You didn't say anything while you were out shopping with Ireland!"

"What would I say?"

"You know damn well what I mean."

"No, not this time."

"You're pushing your luck." But she did think it would be nice to have a man in her life who thought she needed pampering from time to time. No man had ever treated her like this. She was thinking of how nice it was to be waited on. All this personal attention was turning her to jelly. That willful look he'd given her—she hoped he hadn't used it with another woman.

For their wedding breakfast, Chandler prepared everything with great care. Knives, forks, bowls, and even the plates had been properly placed on the cloth covering the white table beneath. The ham and eggs had been cooked to perfection. Even the crescent rolls had been warmed in the oven with a fresh butter coating, and a glass of warm tea waited with the delicate aroma of freshly brewed tea.

Famished, both Sofia and Chandler started to eat.

It was pleasant, having a cheerful man sitting opposite her. Sofia was very pleased with his culinary skills. Some of her energy returned and she was beginning to feel more like her natural, happy self again. After her second cup of tea, she felt some kindness toward Chandler.

Strangely, she felt peaceful. Nevertheless, their situation was complicated. Chandler made Sofia feel a way she'd never thought could be possible.

"What are we going to do?" Finally, a soft, happy feeling was screaming to come out of her voice. "You've put me in an embarrassing situation. Everyone, including my neighbors, now thinks I'm married. Knowing my boss, it won't be long before he spreads the news far and wide through the company. I'm sure he'll phone my aunt and tell her. She's probably in quite a state by now. And poor Jasper . . . how he must be feeling—all because of you." Her glass clunked against her lower teeth.

Chandler took a long drink from his glass and leaned across the table, "This wasn't all my fault—there was a little help from you, too, dear. When you were asked you if you were Madame Riggs, you could have said no."

"You bastard, I had no idea things would ever get this far.

I didn't want you to be embarrassed when you were behaving so proper with me. And I certainly didn't expect my boss to be on the same freaking train, much less be standing right behind me. Why didn't you tell him the whole thing was a joke after we were off the train?"

"I was hoping, for whatever reason, that you would, but you seemed to be having a good time." Chandler smiled as he turned to look at her.

"A good time! I was in a panic! I tried to tell him in the car, but I couldn't, not with you sitting right there. You are broke, remember, and I thought it would have been humiliating for you for whatever reason. And, can you do anything but smile all the damn time?"

Chandler opened his eyes wide. "Why, you shouldn't allow yourself to get in such a tizzy over this. These things happen to the best of people."

"I'm going to act like I didn't hear that. Anyway, you have no idea . . . I thought that once we were back, you would leave. I would explain the whole thing to him later, when the atmosphere was a little calmer. Mind you, it wouldn't have been easy. After all, we did sleep in the same compartment together, but not together. By rearranging a few details, I could have managed to clear the whole thing up. But now . . . he has seen you come up here with me, and if he was to learn you weren't my husband, I'm sure he'd fire me. And I like my job, mind you, not only that I need my job!" Sofia was confused. Tears began to fall. She was fighting to keep her vulnerability from showing.

"Your boss is that much of a bully?"

"He's not a bully—he's old-fashioned and absolutely opposed to this kind of thing. The work I do is very important to me, and I know I wouldn't keep my job long if he ever learned of what I had done."

"You can stop worrying. As soon as I finish this excellent

breakfast, I'll take off and you'll never see me again."

Sofia's mind was fluttering, her brain spinning. The situation proved full of frustrating problems. Sofia looked at him, horrified, a deep chill running down her back. Deep down, she didn't want him to leave, especially not now—she wanted to make love with him. She wanted to know what he felt like. If he were to leave, she would never experience it. Chandler made her feel a way she didn't even know she was capable of.

Her composure always slipped a little when his gaze fell on her, leaving her feverish and awkward under his careless regard. When he was near, she found herself tongue-tied, and intelligent answers came hard, especially when she was angry.

Silence descended for a moment. His words were shocking. Sofia had never heard him speak like that. Her mouth fell open and she stared at him intently. "Chandler, you can't do that! It's too late. How do you think it would make me look—abandoned after only two days of marriage!" Sofia's throat tightened. She could hardly bear the agony of not seeing him again.

He continued smiling. "What would Madame Taxon think?"

He seemed to be very concerned about his reputation with her. He was impeccably groomed, as always, and so handsome he made women feel weak just looking at him.

Chandler continued, "Well, at this point, it isn't really that important. You agree that this situation is no laughing matter. Incidentally, how did you know I wasn't married . . . or engaged?"

Sofia frowned. "Are you?"

"No, thank heavens. I haven't reached the point where I see myself tied to one person."

Without knowing why, Sofia was relieved to hear he

wasn't married or engaged, either. "I'm happy you're single. I would have felt badly about having to take you away from someone else." She sighed contentedly.

"You mean you want to take me away?"

"I—" She blushed. "Only for a while. But—are you free? What do you do for a living? That is, if you don't mind me asking?"

"Just about anything to keep afloat," Chandler replied with a smirk of his smile.

She wanted him, but not at a price she couldn't afford. She answered his question with another question. "Where do you plan to sleep tonight?" She wanted him. He could sleep with her. If she were to approach a man first, what would his thoughts be?

"I believe there are lots of hotels in Paris," he replied.

That wasn't an answer she'd hoped for. "A hotel? You have less than two francs to your name, and you're going to a hotel? You couldn't afford a bed at a mission. Besides, I have a spare room."

They looked intensely at each other. The room was filled with the essence of body heat. Sofia could feel perspiration forming beneath her clothes.

"Two hundred francs a month. Pay me if you can—and if you can't, I don't really care." She let her hormones take over, not her head.

"I get it. You want me to stay here so you can continue to pass me off as your husband. Maybe for a month or so . . . then, you can charge me with mental cruelty—that seems to be the popular way these days—and then file for divorce. Or better still, you can apply for an annulment. And you'll be the poor, innocent victim. Did I miss anything?"

He was only right about a couple of his suggestions. "I hadn't thought that far, but it all sounds pretty good."

"You mean ridiculous! As far as I'm concerned, it's

absurd!"

For a second, Chandler's look was disquieting. Then his eyes grew warm as he spoke in a soft and kind tone. He turned to look at her. "How old are you?"

"Twenty-three. Why?" A flood of self-consciousness made the blood rush to her face. Had Chandler been sizing her up all the time she was evaluating him? She must have come across like an idiot. She'd have to use a little levity to throw him out if she wanted.

"You look sixteen, and right now, you're thinking like a ten-year-old. You think you're in a compromising position, and if I were to move in here, you'd really be in a mess! One of these days, you're going to want to really get married and then you'll have to tell the truth. What will your fiancé think?"

"I don't want Jasper, and if I did, you wouldn't be where you're standing."

"It isn't this Jasper fellow. The same goes for whoever you decide to marry." He stared at her intently.

"Not if he's less conventional, less old-fashioned. Besides, if he loves me, he'll believe me."

"Men in love can be very jealous." His jaw tightened a little.

"But there won't be any reason for him to be jealous of you."

"Look, we both know this, but will he know? Will any-body? Right now, you think you have the answers, but when the time comes, you'll find you don't."

"Right now, all I'm interested in, Chandler, as I told you before, is that I don't want to lose my job." *Sofia lives by her own rules, and hers alone.*

"You can find another job."

"Not like this one. It's a sound business. My boss was a good friend of my parents and he has a lot of confidence in me. I don't want to give security up over something like this." Sofia lifted her head and continued. She noticed with satisfaction that, for a moment, Chandler looked as much at a loss. "If you were to leave now, I'd be the laughingstock of the entire neighborhood and the people I work with. It's like having morals."

"Morals!" He spouted off, "I'm not interested in morals."

Unable to conceal her emotions any longer, Sofia laid her head on the table and wept aloud. If the clock could be turned back, how different life could be! "Call it anything you like, but I've always hated the idea of having people laughing at me. If you were to leave, I don't think I could live with the humiliation . . ." Her voice trembled. "I'd rather die." She shook her head in anguish. "Nothing could be worse. Chandler, you have to help me out of this." She thought quickly. "I helped you out on the train—now it's your turn!"

What kind of stranger was he? Whirling with a mixture of rage, frustration, and humiliation, Sofia flashed a quick look at him from beneath her downcast lashes and caught sight of his gaze on her, but this time his startlingly blue eyes wore a somber, almost thoughtful expression. *What is he thinking?*

Feeling lost and helpless, she went on hurriedly, "One month. That's not very long. I wasn't the one who approached you. You came to me, remember? You're responsible for this. If you have any decency at all, you'll do whatever you can to repair the damage . . . unless, of course, you're afraid to!"

"No, no, I'm not afraid to do anything," Chandler replied, his voice soft. He showed no sign of anger. "I may be a lot of things, but a coward isn't one of them. Don't be so belligerent. If you really wanted me to go, I'd be gone well before now."

These last words irritated Sofia. "I want no such thing,"

she replied indignantly. "Do you really think I'm desperate for a husband?"

Chandler laughed. "At least you don't beat around the bush, darling. I understand how you feel. To marry a man without a penny, without a worthwhile job, a vagabond, you might say. I can see how that wouldn't be very appealing."

Sofia had detected a slight accent in his speech. She smiled at him in confusion. Neither his appearance, his manner, nor his mode of dress corresponded with his description of himself.

"You're not French, are you?"

"I'm a citizen of the world. I have traveled far and wide and speak many languages. But if you really want to know, my father is British, and my mother is French. Does that make any difference with you?"

"No, none of the sort. Will you stay?" she asked smugly, a teasing glint shone in her eye.

He pondered on the question and looked at her earnestly. "It's up to you," Chandler said finally. "You must know I find your offer extremely tempting."

"Naturally," Sofia said scornfully. "You'll have the free room with large windows, hot and cold running water and all the comforts of home."

Chandler's blue eyes mocked her. "Will I have to clean my own room myself?"

"I have a cleaning lady who comes in once a week. She'll be in tomorrow. Speaking of that"—Sofia hesitated, brows drawn inward—"what does that have to do with it? Are you allergic to cleaning up after yourself?"

"I'll make my bed each morning, so no one will ever know I'm not sleeping with my lovely wife, and don't you forget to put four pillows on your bed."

Sofia blushed and answered without thinking, "It already had two pillows, and it's a rather large bed."

"And where shall I eat?"

"In restaurants, and make sure no one finds out!"

"Okay, I'll stay for one month, but I'm not promising to stay any longer," he replied. "You seem to have everything figured out. Honestly, don't you think it would be better if I just went away and never came back?"

She wanted him now, and the atmosphere was set. "With the predicament you have put me in, you owe me, and I intend to collect, one way or another."

For a moment Sofia was tired of hearing his voice. She faced him, her mind racing. He clearly knew what she wanted immediately and his sudden change in manner took her completely. His mouth came down on hers, crushing her lips fiercely under his, and she returned the passion with her body, leaning into his deeply and hungrily, relishing the feel of his hard muscles, He was warm and inviting.

He stared at her with an amused expression. "You really are remarkable. Did you know that? Just the right combination of frivolity and seriousness, confidence and rebellion, fear and daring. I wouldn't ever want to do anything to offend you, Sofia."

His mouth hung loosely, his gaze transfixed on her face. He was willing, urging her to continue to explore. He was taking her lips to his desire to wrap with warm moist strokes, tight then lose and tight again with her tongue stroking him before his hands slipped around her neck and he had to force himself to stop her and take control before all vanished. He took Sofia tight within his arms as his hunger grew, watching her in desperation. He stepped back as she slowly and seductively stripped before his hungry eyes. He sighed in enjoyment as she touched him.

Touching him was more pleasurable than anything she had ever done.

Chandler took full possession of her—all of her. She pressed her hands into his back and felt the tenseness of his muscles, the tautness of his body. Little sounds escaped his mouth, soft words from the depths of his being.

The silence enfolded them. She wanted to please him as he pleased her. Little by little she drifted back to the night she was attracted by his appearance.

She returned his kisses in a way she had never dreamed. She stared at him dreamily. "It's wonderful, isn't it? Feeling this way?" Sofia felt him softly brush her cheek with his hand, then he found her lips with his again, softly at first, changing to an aggressive forcefulness. She felt his strength, the power of his arms around her, and in that moment, she knew it could never stop. Sofia started with the top button of her blouse, and continued button by button until there were none. Both his hands were firmly over her breasts, caressing her flesh gently while his mouth plowed into the smooth, soft bareness of her body, over and over, until her excitement could not be contained.

She reached for him, gliding her fingers along his firm naked skin. Her desire for him became the strongest sensation she had ever known. In her mind there was nothing ahead of them, nothing behind them.

She wanted to discover everything about him. She was bold and aggressive with her hands, seeking the source of his greatest desire, concentrating on it, experimenting with a new freedom that almost frightened her. The thought burst across her mind—she could do anything she wanted with him.

Opening her eyes, she marveled to herself at the beauty of his body. She came up to a sitting position, her gaze slowly traveling the length of him stretched out beside her body. She wanted to please him as he pleased her.

She stared at him happily.

Slowly he raised himself up and took her face in both his hands, bending close to her mouth. "This is the way love is, Sofia. There's nothing evil about it." Chandler lead her to the bedroom where he kissed her passionately while lowering her to the bed, moaning softly against her mouth.

Her lips quivered, and she felt the shaking start inside her. His chest joined hers and she stirred beneath him as his kiss widened, his touch darting in and out. His kiss hardened, then his tongue ran over her teeth and captured hers in a long, savoring curl. A throaty cry escaped her as he sank carefully down, covering her body with his warm flesh.

A sense of being alive came to her as never before, filling her with cravings for him. In his arms she was truly at peace with herself, and with the world. This was love, the feeling inside her. It had come to her. For once in her life something wonderful beyond words had happened to her. She would make it stay this way forever.

Sofia caught her breath sharply, feeling the chill of flames move up her legs and down her body to meet in a soaring blaze, reaching beyond her.

She held her breath, feeling as though a wonderful discovery was on its way. She liked the way Chandler made her feel like she was wanted. She released a low moan as he took her. With a soft cry she twisted her body so that she stood free of him, eyeing him through a veil of delirium. She extended the tip of her tongue between her teeth as she fastened her gaze unblinkingly to his.

Sofia let out a shout—he was huge, and she could barely take him. As he pushed, he kept sliding her on the bed until she was on all fours. The more she cried out, the harder he became until finally, he was on the bed with her, pulling her body back to him fast and hard as he buried himself deeper inside her. She writhed and began to shudder. She wasn't sure whether the feelings were pleasure or pain, so strong in intensity they were. She was tingling, vibrating all over, and it was a moment of strange frustration, as if she were desperate, exposed as she had never been. But, she loved every moment.

Chandler was close, and Sofia knew it. She knew it, and felt it, as he hardened even more, throbbing in tune with his heartbeat as he exploded inside her, deep and heavy.

Sofia's face was flushed and her mouth was dry. "You must have a lot of women in your life." She already knew in her mind what his answer to that foolish question would be, but she wanted to hear the answer from Chandler, not her mind.

Chandler had to think about it before answering. He smiled at her tenderly. "What does it matter? One, or a dozen? It shouldn't matter to you. Have I asked you how many lovers you've had?"

Without answering he changed immediately and ripped her panties from her, ultimately shredding them. He turned her around to face the bed, then wrapped one arm around her stomach and bent her over, holding her in place with his other hand while standing at the edge of the bed. "You are so beautiful!" he whispered, then reached back and placed his hand between her legs, probing until he found her sweet spot. Every part of her was vulnerable to him, to his fire, and little by little she felt her muscles slacken as a muffled cry escaped her.

Chandler collapsed on top of her, squeezing her tight within his arms, pressing his head into her neck, breathing deeply as if he just finished a run. Then abruptly the threshold separating them was invaded and she pushed out a long harsh moan.

It took Chandler a moment or so to pull out. He clearly needed a little bit to get his composure back, but Sofia didn't mind. They both lay unmoving, breathing hard, until they were aware again of the room surrounding them.

If she had known she would get a reply like this she would have asked the question over and over.

CHAPTER THREE

Sofia hoped Chandler understood that she ran her own life, and no man was going to step in and change it, unless it was to her liking.

Each moment, each incident, taken on its own, had very little strength. Like single threads, they could be severed. A tapestry, however, was nearly impossible to tear. In barely three days, Sofia and Chandler had laughed together, cried together and shared the light of day. They danced like lovers and played like children. Sofia found happiness. Never had a man gotten to her like Chandler. The thoughts never left her mind. *There's got to be something more to him, her handsome stranger in the night.* Sofia continued to study him hard.

"Just a simple arrangement, between the two of us, right?" Chandler observed, smiling wickedly.

"Yes, just a simple arrangement." Sofia was good with the *simple arrangement,* but she wanted to share his bed in a more permanent agreement.

"Now, unfortunately, I must leave you. As I said last night, I have an important meeting this morning." Chandler stood up to leave the table and looked at the dirty dishes. "Do you want some help with those before I leave?"

"No, thanks. I'll get them later, besides, that's what a dishwasher is for. There aren't many, but I appreciate the thought." *Did he just offer to do her dishes? Am I in a dream?* One thing started to weigh heavily on her mind. A perfect stranger who happened to have fallen right into her lap, her bed, and wanted to help with the dishes. Did the guy have some sort of life, friends, family to contact on his whereabouts? Places to be? People to see? So many questions with no answers to follow.

With a deep breath, Sofia clung to her private thoughts and pushed him out the door. The more she thought about Chandler, it always led to sex. Could she be in love with him, or infatuated with the sex? Either way, she wanted more, no matter what the cost or consequence.

"You're sure? I'll be happy to help you." Chandler started inching his way slowly to the door, then quickly turned around. "I hope I don't disturb you when I get back. It'll be around nine or so . . . unless, you want to give me a key. You wouldn't have to get up and open the door for me."

Sofia had to think about the answer. She wasn't sure what she wanted to do. The only thing she was sure of was that she had experienced the best sex she'd ever had.

"Come here," Chandler demanded softly, his mouth willing, his touch urging her to continue, to explore.

Sofia, in return, kissed his lips in a way she had never kissed another man before, freely, blissfully. Without hesitation she followed his command. She felt one of his hands brush her cheek, then his mouth again found her lips, softly at first, changing to an aggressive forcefulness. Almost instantly, she blazed as if she had been burned. She felt his strength, the power of his arms around her, and in that moment, she knew it would never stop.

Sofia could feel the quiver of his lips throughout her body. She felt the warmth of his hands, his fingers pressing into her back. She was feeling a strange off-balance sensation gripping her as though an invisible breeze was swaying her. She couldn't stop if she wanted, and that moment she felt almost frightened by the intensity of her feelings. Hardly able to breathe, she pulled her mouth from his control.

"I knew I shouldn't have started this," Chandler whispered in her ear. "I must go," he implored.

Sofia knew he had somewhere he needed to be, and she didn't urge him to stay longer.

Chandler wanted a key to her apartment. She had never given anyone a key. She looked in one drawer, then another and finally, in the back of a side drawer, she found one, but she was unsure if it was one to her door, and she put it atop her dresser. *If he keeps his end of the bargain and comes back, it's his.*

Sofia couldn't think of anything else. She paced back and forth, talking to herself. "Damn it, he's so great in bed. He won't come back. Men like him rarely do. I have nothing to offer, unless ten franks are a lot to have in the bank, then it's right up his alley."

What was I thinking? How could I have been caught up in a situation like this? I should have said no on the train and sent him on his way. He could be a serial killer for all I know. I should have had my head damn examined to have gone along with this.

Her thoughts flitted back to the moment when Chandler took her, cupping her face within his palms, staring deeply into her eyes, before pressing his lips to hers. Sofia felt desire and knew what it meant. She had tasted it on her lips, felt it in her body, relived it in her mind over and over. She had never known it, until now, and knew she could not live without it.

Could Chandler walk away from her, or could she ever allow it? Tension had been building between them. Chandler had the right recipe, and Sofia was the ingredient.

Chandler was remarkable, and Sofia felt herself being drawn by his charm like a fly to a web. And although he wasn't there to hold her hand, she still felt powerless to pull away.

Suddenly the doorbell rang. "Who could this be?" Sofia whispered. She flung the door open and Chandler stepped in. Smiling at her, he must have known immediately from the way she was responding she couldn't resist him. He must have wanted her as much as she did him, to have returned so quickly. Her mind was racing, rendering her incapable of speech.

Looking at his face was like looking directly into the sun, bringing her to a feeling of absolute warmth and radiance. She put her mouth to his and they kissed over and over until they both trembled and gasped to breathe. His lips left her mouth and brushed across the side of her face and down her throat.

"You will always come back to me, won't you, Chandler?" Sofia demanded in a groan. "Tell me you will always come back," in the kiss that followed his words. In this moment everything, everyone, became meaningless.

Hand in hand they entered the bedroom, collapsing in a withering embrace on the side of her bed. He lowered himself above her, pressing her down until her head lay on the pillow. Gazing at her, into her luminous eyes, he told her in soft words, "I want you so much. I can't think of anything else. I haven't thought of anyone since I met you."

Happiness appeared in her smile. "You have me Chandler. I'll be yours anytime you want me."

He didn't move but remained motionless, a gentle expression on his face. "I'm falling in love with you, Sofia. Did you know that?" He traveled his gaze down Sofia's slender body and then up again

She pressed her body pressed ever so lightly against him. She looked up into his eyes, brushed his chin with her lips.

Opening her mouth, she reached for his lips, hurling them together in a suffocating embrace. She returned his kisses with a whole heart, a whole being. He wove his hands into her hair as her nails dug through the shirt he wore, clinging to him. She didn't want to let him go, not even for an instant. It was happening. She dared not let go for fear he would change his mind. She held him captive with her arms, and with her mouth. Her lungs labored for air.

Chandler invaded Sofia's mouth with his own, wetting her lips as his tongue joined hers in an exquisite pleasure that spun golden blood through her veins. He pulled away and she lay back, watching the precision of his hands as he took off his clothes. Then he lowered himself toward her and loosened the cloth belt of her robe. She could feel his erection pressed tightly against her. She savagely went for him, kissing his chest while he guided the hard desire of his erection downward to the warmth of her soft lips as he plunged deep in her mouth.

His thighs were rock hard against her shoulder blade, his hand a lead weight holding her at his feet, his head and should looming above her to keep her from rising. She was caught in his trap like a fly in a web, yet to all outward appearances she kneeled lovingly at his feet and was happy to have his hand on her head.

"The morning is ours," he whispered as he loomed over her, cupping her head to stroke in and out of her mouth, as if he was making love to her lips. He threw his head back with his eyes pressed shut, whispering, "oh, yeah," then "ohhhhhhh, if you don't stop, I'm going to come in your mouth." He reached deep and pulled out in just the right second, his breathing excited.

Sofia arched back into her pillow when she felt his mouth touching her stomach, her body, and with one swift move she welcomed him. Cold chills were taunting her, her nipples hardening, perfect for the picking while he savored the moment. Chandler twined a handful of her hair through his fingers and strongly tilted Sofia's head back, exposing her tender flesh. He slowly made long, warm and moist streaks with his tongue along her neck, stripping away her restraint. Sofia was purring like a kitten as Chandler explored body with feather light strokes.

Chandler seized her breasts, taking one hard nipple amidst his teeth, teasing and suckling, while cupping and caressing the other with his fingers. Sofia was urging him on—she wanted more, matching his rhythm to let him know how great he made her feel. She could feel her heart beating inside her chest and reeled with a wicked delight.

Chandler released her to roll her over to mount and took his fill, unshackling his lust, slowly at first and then speeding up.

Sofia was breathing heavily and with no control. She gave in to his need. She was moaning as she began to pant, on all fours for a second time. Sofia was tight, and she knew she wouldn't hold out long.

He eased over her right shoulder, meeting her with a tiny grin on his face. He pushed her face sideways on the pillow with a fistful of hair, pulling her head back again with half his strength. Sofia cried out with every thrust. It felt so good, and she didn't want him to stop, so she begged for more, knowing he liked it deep and hard.

Chandler was raw and primitive with a searing need. He wasn't like any other boyfriend she'd had. He was intoxicating. Who was this man, to command without a single word?

Waves of euphoria coursed through Sofia's veins as she encouraged more. She couldn't get enough of him. Sofia could barely hold him back. She knew he couldn't hold it in any longer, and the same for her, she didn't plan it this way. His erection grew harder as he molded himself in her for a dual, shattering climax. Chandler laid on top of her for a minute to get his composure back, before making a mad dash for the shower.

"That was the best ten minutes I've ever had," Sofia commented. "I'm sorry if I made you late for your appointment." The kiss confounded her, it felt like farewell for some reason. It was a thought she was not completely sure she should have been thinking.

"They can start without me," Chandler replied from the shower. "Besides, it's just a few minutes. It won't hurt a thing."

Sofia checked and rechecked the room Chandler would be using, to make sure everything was in order. True, he was penniless, but he had the air of a man who was used to the finer things. This Sofia noticed on the train.

The relationship wouldn't last if the sex wasn't any good, and Chandler was up for anything Sofia liked, no matter how erotic it may have been. He was the cause of this, she thought. She wanted him to be happy while he was staying with her, since he had agreed to help her out—help her through a situation that she would never have thought could happen to her, and wouldn't have if her boss hadn't sent her on that train. The only reason she wouldn't throw him out, was because she wanted him around for the sex, and he was the best she had ever had.

She had a good feeling about him, more than just lusting after his gorgeous ass and the sex. If it had been anyone else, would Sofia have allowed him to share her empty berth? It depended on what they looked like. And yet, there was something about Chandler that was different from anyone she had ever known. It was hard to know what to make of Chandler, after spending time with him.

There were obviously more layers to Chandler than Sofia had at first suspected, but which of them figured predominantly in his personality? She couldn't quite determine. She was willing to admit she might have imagined him in a different light. But the sex, she kept going back for it. He was remarkably wonderful. No other man had ever made her feel the way she felt for Chandler. Then, with a sudden flash of clarity, she had things to do.

Sofia smiled. In the past, she spent her holidays with her parents. After they'd passed away she would visit Jasper's parents in the north of France. It all seemed so dreary now. No wonder her time in Nice had been so marvelous. For the first time, she felt like she was really having a holiday. She had laughed and enjoyed herself, and for once in her life she felt free and uninhibited. Despite the strangeness of her situation, she felt the same way with Chandler. She was happy in his presence and exuberant when he looked at her. Perhaps that was the reason she'd opened her berth for him that night. The way they met, that would never happen to her a second time. She was falling in love with Chandler.

Sofia spent the afternoon running errands, shopping and just enjoying being out without restraints. The weather was hit or miss—one day it may be beautiful, perfect weather and the next nothing but rain. When in the park she loved to feed the pigeons. Everyone knows a pigeon never forgets anything, especially when they're fed, and who feeds them. Sofia had her favorites.

She really didn't believe he would come back, and thought, since he was away, she would be back to the way things were in no time. Sofia knew men often would say anything to be with a woman, and especially when they wanted no strings attached. She was stronger than most women her age, and making it on her own, she was doing quite well. But she was in love, and didn't want to live alone any longer.

Chandler had explained that he would leave and be gone until late at night, long after she would usually retire. She really wasn't pleased with this part of the agreement.

Later that evening there was a knock on the door and Sofia answered it, surprised. Like a deer in headlights, she

stood almost frozen when she saw it was him. She hadn't
expected Chandler to come back. Why would he, really?
Maybe for the sex? He could move in right now, if it was just
for that. Losing the best sex she had ever had would be a
bummer.

"What, something wrong?" he asked, while struggling
with his arms packed with bags overfilled with groceries.
"Doesn't a husband get a warm welcoming when he comes
home from being out all day?" he commented, smiling.
"And to find a lovely, smiling wife waiting. You see, I came
back. You could have given me a key. No matter what you
may think, I really am quite honest, and you must admit,
very punctual. Here is the ten francs you lent me this morning, plus two hundred francs for my rent. Count it if you
like. And if I don't stay the full month, you can keep it, anyway. Like you said, it's only money."

Sofia followed him into the living room and watched in
wonderment as he put the bills on the table. "Where did you
get all that damn money?" she demanded angrily. After
what he had done to her, to let everyone think they were
married, and the day before he'd been broke, couldn't afford
as much as buy a ticket to get home, and had to beg her for a
berth to sleep in.

"In Paris, there are any number of ways to get money. I
may not look like it, but I'm very astute, as well as practical.
If you need more money, just say the word. I'll be glad to
lend it to you."

"Lend it to me? Lend it to me!" Sofia repeated, spewing
her words across the room. "I don't need your damn money,
you got that?" She pointed an angry finger right between his
eyes. "And I mean it. Sex isn't worth it—I don't have to have
anything from any man." Stomping across the floor, she
nearly wore out a trail in five minutes. "Chandler, what have
you been up to?" she demanded with a tilt of her head in a

loud whisper.

"Nothing that a resourceful man without a penny in his pocket wouldn't do. You mustn't think your husband went out and robbed a bank or something. Even if it were true, I wouldn't want you to be thinking it."

Even when he was acting silly, he lost nothing of his distinguished look. Sofia felt like slapping that smirk right off his face. "Can't you ever be serious about anything?"

"I can't stand serious people. Just be happy. You have a happy husband who believes the whole universe was created for his pleasure, so don't look so shocked."

"It's just . . . no one's ever spoken to me like this." Although the reality was, she'd never known anyone quite like Chandler.

"Usually husbands and wives kiss each other goodnight, but I guess that's not part of the deal?" Chandler seemed to be unaffected by the whole situation. He continued putting the groceries away as if nothing was going on. "Ah, my dear, you should really loosen up and live without all the stress. Your life would be better if you did. Now, I don't want to keep you from what you were doing. I think I'm going to turn in early. It's been a long day." He smiled.

Oh, how terribly bad she was, but she desperately wanted to kiss him. Could he see it in her eyes? Surely, or why would he say such a thing?

"Maybe after we get to know each other a little better," she whispered.

"I believe we have gotten to know one another, don't you think?" he said, "Oh, darling, just one more small detail. Is there a lock on my door?" There seemed to be an old-fashioned discipline about him.

Sofia answered, "Of course there is a fine lock on your door." How could she sleep after that? Wanting to know about the lock. Had this guy lost his mind? She halfway thought he would want her to share his bed after what they had been through in such a short time.

"Great! Because, you see, I don't know anything about you, either. And if you can be afraid of strange men, certainly I can be just as afraid of strange women. Especially strange women as charming as you."

With that, Chandler turned on his heel and strolled quickly to his room.

Sofia wanted to take off after him, body slam him onto his bed, strip off her clothing and ravish his luscious loins inch by hungry inch. The only problem was that it was merely taking place within the comforts of her thoughts.

Women weren't made for the life Chandler Riggs led. He did think it might be kind of nice to think of keeping Sofia, but he knew it was neither practical nor fair. It had struck Chandler what a good wife Sofia would make, then in the same instant, he'd shocked with himself for having such a thought. Chandler Riggs needed no wife. Having a woman around would be handy, but not something a man like himself would want all the time. He had to move around, and sometimes be alone.

He hadn't had this much turmoil in his life in years. *See what happens when a man lets himself get involved with a woman?* And what bothered him most was that he was attracted to her. His mind was filled to overflowing with her—her face, her body, the delightful way tiny dimples appeared at the corners of her mouth when she smiled. The way she said his name.

He could never let himself grovel over her. His pride was valuable to him. His head ached, and he couldn't help but wonder if it was brought on by the painful frustration from this strange woman with velvet eyes. His heart felt heavy and he was now confused. He'd never wanted a woman before, not like this.

He always thought he'd be forced by fate into settling, like the average man, but he couldn't picture such a thing, and he suddenly started thinking about it all. Chandler sighed and rested his head, closing his eyes for a moment. A thousand thoughts rushed through his mind at once as he lay quietly in the dark. He had nothing solid to support himself or her. Men like him were a dying breed.

It was getting to him that he remembered the grace of Sofia's movement, the smell of her body, and the softness of her hair. There was something innocent and sweet about her. It was as though he was free of all thoughts of anything bad or sinful when everything reminded him of her. Chandler shook his head, disgusted with himself for entertaining such thoughts. He closed his eyes again, his hand across his forehead.

There was something different about her, this much he knew to be a fact. What now bothered him the most was that he had a serious attraction to Sofia. Confusion over a woman whom he just met was new to him. Chandler was not a one-woman man—he liked his freedom and his women.

Through the darkness, the first ray of moonlight began to appear while silence hung over the room, then suddenly, he heard a tap on his door. It was Sofia. What could she possibly be wanting? not that it didn't run through his mind what he was hoping to happen. Slowly, he reached for the handle of his door, thinking she was going to blurt something out before he could get the door even open.

"Yes?" He hesitated when their eyes locked. "Ah," was all he could muster up before nearly swallowing his tongue.

She wanted him, all right—right then, and right there. Sofia drew a deep, hard breath, then steadied her voice to say, "I couldn't sleep." Sofia looked at him with a smile, then she shifted as she opened her robe and slipped it off her shoulders. There she stood, sex dripping from her loins, and curves to take any man off his mind.

Sofia's gaze met Chandler's. She stared for several long seconds, her eyes never changing, her breathing quickening.

Chandler's needs outweighed the odds and would not allow him to turn her away. He looked at Sofia's lovely face, his breath soft and wanting, as if he didn't care one way or another what anyone felt, but he neither paused nor hesitated. The distance between them narrowed as Chandler leaned forward, taking her into his arms with such a force that Sofia never pulled away.

Chandler moved his hand around and brushed her hair from her face. Almost instantly a fire ripped through his aching loins, and all his senses, desires coming alive as lust consumed him. There was no turning back.

"I didn't think a woman could be this beautiful," Chandler whispered as he kissed her soft skin that wrapped her tender face. Suddenly, he took Sofia into his arms, parting her lips, searching for the passion she possessed, yearning for the warmth her body radiated.

A silence filled the room and she swallowed hard, keeping her gaze averted. She knew his affections had warmed again, and her heart refused to slow to a regular beat.

His voice, when he spoke, was low and rich with passion. "Come here, Sofia."

She froze. She would stay where she was. Her happiness was presented in full countenance, and a smile softened his face. She unthinkingly placed a hand upon his chest, and the touch was electric.

Their gazes met and held, and the smiles faded. His hands seemed to finish their task of their own accord, then, as if moved by some other force, they slid over her shoulders to her back, almost pressing her to him. Sofia felt very weak. Her legs began to tremble, and breathing was almost impossible. But still his gaze held her prisoner, and in the room, time seemed to stop, as if suspended or paused.

His eyelids lowered, and he smiled slowly. "I admire your spirt."

Sofia shook. Her legs were trembling, her teeth tugging at her lower lip as she stood in his arms. She couldn't resist him. He smiled at her leisurely, and, sliding his hand up her arm, pulled her between his legs.

He moved his mouth over her shaking lips and parted them as he slid his arm around her, one hand on her back, while he sought her hip with the other. With a half cry, Sofia went limp against his chest, trembling within his grasp. His kisses went on, it seemed to her, without end. When his hand slid from her hip to her thigh and moved slowly upward along the inside, caressing it, she groaned under his kiss and strained against his chest. But the embrace could not be broken. His lips left hers to kiss the corners of her mouth, her chin, her ear.

His kisses traveled down her neck to the rounded curves of her flesh. He caressed her breasts unhurriedly, moving from the deep valley between to the pointed peaks which rose up. His breath came more rapidly and touched her skin like a hot iron.

Sofia threw her head back, smiling, hugging his head as his soft, moist lips left a trail of warmth, as his tongue moved down, as he took one hard nipple in his teeth, nibbling gently while he moved his hands down her back and over her bare hips. Chandler's instincts wouldn't let him stop. It was thrilling to taste her, to run his hands over every curve and hollow.

Sofia pulled him inside her in the most perfect way. She closed her eyes as she gasped and moved rhythmically with him as he felt her tremble. She arched upward, pulsating spasms pulling him deeper. She took him so beautifully.

Sofia snuggled up to him as if it was natural and right. What had just taken place left behind a calling card. Chandler had a feeling Sofia was in love. Maybe it was the sex.

Sofia was beautiful, and making love made her happy. She'd taken him with such sweet abandonment. She was wearing nothing but his shirt. The pain of guilt sliced through him like a sharp blade and came back. He'd made love to a beautiful woman for no reason other than his own needs. He loved her—everything about her.

His skin was hot and tingly. His fingers explored forbidden places, finding a velvety moistness. Chandler slid his hand between her legs as her breathing quickened. Guilt and honor couldn't overcome her beauty and his needs. He lifted Sofia into his arms and consumed her lips as he carried her to his bed, laying her down, then finished releasing her from any attire she had left.

Chandler shuddered with delight as he moved his lips over her throat and down to the succulent fruit of her breast, struggling to keep from moving too fast. Chandler lightly teased her flesh, gently caressing her breast and drawing its sweetness into his mouth, his heart beating furiously, taking his liberties without objection. He held on until it was impossible to stop the surge of life that spilled out in response to the heavenly sensations she had created within him. He moved his hands along her satiny skin, up and over her desire. He toyed with one nipple, the agony of wanting her tearing through him in pulsing waves of passion. He wanted to ravage her, be wild with her. He sank to his knees, running his hands over her thighs and lifting her hips, drinking in her utter beauty as she stood before him.

Chandler was lost in silken rapture, moving harshly. He reached under Sofia's hips, grasping them firmly, pushing into her with moans of ecstasy. There was an animal lust. Being inside her flooded him with shuddering hunger.

"Don't stop!" she demanded.

Chandler pulled away from her, a heavy feeling in his chest. What was this woman doing to him? And what was this feeling in him that made him feel that he wanted to keep her forever? He lay down, pulling her into his arms and drawing the sheet over them, and as soon as her breasts moved against his bare flesh he knew he wouldn't make it through the night without making love to her again.

Chandler woke at dawn. His mind was foggy with sleep at first, as he stretched and rubbed at his eyes. His stomach was growling like a grizzly'. He stood and stumbled his way to the bathroom to relieve himself and for some much-needed personal hygiene. He ran his hands through his hair and stretched a second time, thinking of how nice it would be if Sofia were to walk in on him.

His mind was racing with images of the night before—the feel of her tender body next to his, the glory of tasting her sweet breasts, the warmth of silken moistness against his fingers—with ecstasy surging through his veins.

The sun came in rays of sparkling light through the water-speckled window. Now a soft rain-sweetened breeze flirted with a curtain where a window had been left ajar and drifted across the bed to touch his cheek. Chandler inhaled deeply and released his breath with a grateful sigh. The smell of autumn was in the air.

Chandler felt a light tap on his shoulder and turned to see her standing over him with coffee. He accepted the cup, smiling eagerly.

"What's with the look?" Sofia inquired with one brow

drawn inward.

"It's morning." Chandler smiled and walked over to the table and sat down. He was eager for something to eat.

"Don't you go and get all mushy with me. It was just sex. Nothing more," Sofia commented.

"Just sex," Chandler replied. He couldn't believe what his ears were conveying.

"That's right, just sex," Sofia uttered. "It's the twenty-first century, dear, in case you've not noticed. I'm not the marrying kind, and if that surprises you for a woman to talk that way, then you're just going to have to be surprised."

"I, ah . . . I don't know what to say." It floored Chandler—he was speechless and couldn't believe a word of what she just said.

"What is there to say?" Sofia asked. "What's good for the goose is good for the gander these days." She hesitated, as if there was something else she was going to add, but didn't. "I like men, I like sex, and I'm not looking to fall in love, just lust maybe, but love, definitely not so much for now."

Chandler had never heard a woman speak this way, let alone feel this way. He found it appealing. "I totally understand—you're using me for sex."

"Well, I guess you could look at it like that, but nothing's changed as far as our arrangement," she added. "Nothing's changed on that point. This marriage is nothing more than a business arrangement."

"It's just that no woman has ever spoken to me like this before." His true qualities of wit and power left him a bit. There was not a beauty anywhere in the world who had done this to him. She left him speechless, breathless.

"Oh, my dear, you have yet to know what I'm like. I find it very courageous of you, staying here. You know no one, you don't know where anything is, you don't even know the roads and where they lead to. You have your breakfast, and

I have to leave for work," Sofia said quickly. "I don't want to keep you from what you were doing, but I have to go to work. If you go out, don't forget to take my number, it's on the fridge in case you need to reach me. It's my work number and they'll get your call to me. Enjoy your day. I get off at five, and home by six. I have to stop by the store."

"Don't husbands and wives at least kiss one another goodbye?" Chandler smiled.

"Did you not get enough of that last night?" Sofia returned the same smile.

"No, I did not—I want seconds." He gave her a fleeting, searching look. He took a step, then smiled at her.

For a moment everything was breathlessly still in the room. He did not dare meet those eyes of hers. He looked towards the floor.

"Your seconds will have to wait. I have to go to work or I'm going to be late."

Chandler walked away feeling like a kid that didn't get that one toy they just had to have before the world ended.

Chapter Four

Finally, after a few days, Chandler's luggage arrived from Monte Carlo. The leather suitcases were expensive and had his initials, *CR*, engraved on each piece. Now, convinced more than before that Chandler was honest, she gave him a key to her apartment. However, she also wasn't born yesterday. Something was going on, and Chandler wasn't uttering a word about it.

"Thank you, dear," he said. "It would have become quite difficult for me to keep coming home every night at nine. Paris doesn't start to come alive till then. And I don't remember your having asked me to be a faithful husband. I've been too well-brought up to have a young woman wait up for a man all hours of the morning. You're not the jealous type, are you?" Chandler had spoken with the same offhand, slightly impertinent tone he often used with Sofia.

Sofia picked on the word *home*. He'd said when he came home late. She loved it, but she couldn't admit it to him. She simply shrugged without answering. She knew it was written all over her face—she *was* jealous, but she didn't want him to think so. That was right, she was jealous, and she wanted Chandler to herself. Then suddenly she broke her split-second silence, "I don't care what you do in your spare time, if you keep up your end of this deal," she answered. "But, whatever you do, don't let anyone around here see you other than in a *husband* way."

The actuality of the night struck her with a sudden bluntness. A new wave of anger swamped her. Anger directed at herself, at her life. What was she trying to do to him? Did she seriously mean what she had said, or was it a way to say *I love you*? What kind of woman would have sex with a stranger?

What will Madame Taxon think of his nocturnal comings and goings? Who really cares what she thinks, she's just a landlord, no father, no boss. Sofia was a grown woman, paid her own bills, and could do what she wanted.

"Oh, don't worry about her, she's a sound sleeper. And by the way, she snores like a bear. Mind you, I don't know why I just said that, maybe because I don't know a thing about bears. Do you suppose there's terrible lack in my education?"

Sofia frowned. She could see the scenario of a future as if it was playing out right in front of her. "Oh, Chandler, you're impossible. Can't you ever talk seriously about anything?"

"Do I hear a slight bit of jealousy that's not supposed to be there?" He laughed. "Alright, then, let's be serious. Believe me, you don't have to worry about Madame Taxon. There's a list of the names of her tenants tacked to her door. If she should ever wake up and ask who's there, I'd simply tell her I was Monsieur Marx—a delightful name, isn't it— the man who lives on the fourth floor."

Sofia quickly turned around. "You can't do that! Monsieur Marx is a charming old man who works for an insurance firm. He never goes out at night."

"So what if he doesn't go out at night? Besides, he might suddenly have the urge to go out, mightn't he? And if your landlady was to ask about it, I can assure you, if she had to make a choice between the two of us, it would be my word, she'd take me, she's crazy about me."

Sofia didn't doubt it for a minute. Chandler could be utterly charming. He had already enchanted most of the people in the building. But why couldn't he behave like other people occasionally?

"It might not work, Chandler. Your first joke didn't turn out all that well."

"And a good thing, too, my dear. After all, I live by my wits. If it weren't for ideas, I'd be just another ordinary worker, and I don't have that kind of courage. A life tied to a desk would absolutely destroy me."

On those words, Chandler turned and went to his room.

Surely Chandler was exaggerating. Sofia worked at a desk, and *she* didn't feel tied down. She had inherited some money from her parents, but it hadn't been enough for her to be free and independent. Like thousands of other people, she had a job—a well-paid job, too, and in a friendly atmosphere—but a job all the same.

Chandler was absolutely revolting. But he was also the most handsome man she'd laid eyes on. As far as the sex went, she could see herself with him. She had the time of her life. He knew which buttons to push, and right where they were.

But Sofia wasn't going to allow herself to get upset, either. M. Parlay had given her an extra week off to enjoy her honeymoon. Wasn't that a laugh! She might as well take advantage of the free time to see some of the new plays in town and do some shopping for the fall.

Sofia was just about ready to go out when rain started to pepper down, patting lightly against the window panes. She looked outside and saw streams of water already gushing down the streets, giving the roadway a gleaming black sheen. People were running in all directions, trying to find shelter from the sudden downpour.

It was an action story, full of suspense, and kept her on the edge of her seat. Sofia had decided to forget about shopping and went into the bathroom where she washed out two pairs of nylons. Then she had gone to the bookshelf to find one of her favorite authors to read, since it was the right time to cozy up with a great book. She chose a detective novel she had purchased some time back, and she'd been waiting for a chance to read it with no interruptions. For a few hours, Sofia forgot about her problems, having escaped into an imaginary world of mystery and intrigue.

The rain continued, beating on the windowsill in a regular, monotonous rhythm that had an almost numbing effect. Just before five-thirty, Sofia heard Chandler leave the apartment. She made no effort to speak to him. But she couldn't help but to wonder if he was sincere in his word and would even come back, after all this time. She wasn't to be alone for long. The sound of the doorbell startled her. Who could it be at this hour?

Sofia walked over to the door. Much to her surprise, it was Jasper, pale and drawn, his overcoat drenched with rain.

Sofia stood blocking the doorway, but he fiercely pushed her aside and strode right in as if he owned the place.

She shouted, in a flicker of surprise, "Jasper!"

He pushed past Sofia as if the apartment belonged to him. "I believe, Sofia, at the very least, you owe me an explanation."

Sofia was bewildered by his brusque manner.

His discomfort was obvious as he stood awkwardly and avoided her gaze.

She moved away hesitantly, upset by his presence.

"I owe you nothing, and besides, I'm married now. What's the use?" Somehow that sounded strangely comforting to say.

"It all seems very strange to me, dearie. Your boss told me all about how you met this guy on a train—a *train* of all places, Sofia. What were you thinking?" He spoke with a stunned look. "Before you went away for your business trip, we were nearly engaged. And you come back married. What the hell happened?" Jasper's eyes were set in deep, darkened sockets.

He gaped at her, his eyes strained to her. "You didn't waste much time in finding yourself another man, did you?" His frown was now a fierce scowl and his cheek twitched spasmodically.

She took a long time to answer. "I didn't find him. We were on the train together, Jasper."

An absolute silence followed, and he gave a single shake of his head. Finally, he swallowed and said, "And you just happened to fall in love, like with me? Is that it?"

Her head jerked back. She glanced up to find him close beside her. There was an odd look in his eyes, halfway between pain and pleasure, and he looked as if he wanted to speak. He gritted his teeth, and a scowl darkened his features.

He went on. "It's okay. I understand." He considered her pale face. "I know all about him. His name, what he looks like. Everything." He was struggling to speak.

"Is that what you think?" She was so damned happy with her present life, and she'd fight to keep it this way, making his sarcasm hard to ignore.

He threw out one hand, gazing intently at her. "Don't smile about it. I don't find it to be all that amusing."

"Don't blame me for what happened, Jasper," Sofia whispered, her eyes once full of tears. "Look, you don't own me, and honestly, I don't have the feelings strong enough to marry you. It's why I left when I did. It's over, Jasper, and if you do anything—anything—to hurt me or break my relationship up, I will not sit idly by and let you get away with it."

Jaspers shoulders tensed, as did his voice. "How in the

hell did you get in this mess? You're free, damn it. Don't you know what this has done to other people?"

"I don't concern myself with other people's feelings when it comes to who I spend my time and life with. You can tell your friends or family, I don't care which. I live my life by my rules, not yours, not anyone's. Got it?" She flashed him a worried glance.

Unsteady steps took Sofia away from where he stood gaping at her. Then her back stiffened. "I don't want to fight with you, Jasper, do you hear me?"

His face flushed with anger, he yelled, "It's no fight, believe me! It's more than that."

Sofia looked at him in bewildered intensity. "I live my life like I want, not by you or anyone. I met him, and his name is Chandler Riggs, and I love him, Jasper! I love him! I owe you nothing, and I want you gone before this turns into something we'll both regret."

"Are you saying that you were swept off your feet by the first man that came along? Is it?" Jasper demanded. "Answer me, Sofia—is that what you're saying?" His tone was horrifyingly jealous and frightening. He was repeating his words, and when Jasper did that, he could be dangerous and not realize it. He sometimes blacked out and claimed not to be responsible for his actions when he came to. "Come on, Sofia. We both know that's not you. I thought we were a couple!" Spittle sprayed from his lips.

Sofia had been seeing everything differently since meeting Chandler. It was true, but she wasn't exactly sure she was in love with him. That little thing called *lust* kept rolling around in her mind. She was in love with Chandler and didn't know what to do. Love was not something she was ready to allow to be served on a platter. Thoroughly embarrassed and a bit confused, Sofia followed Jasper into the living room and watched as he dropped into her chair, drenched coat and all.

"Do you fucking mind? You are all wet, and you just sat down like it's nothing! Get the hell up before you cause more damage." Sofia was furious—she'd paid for that chair. "That's what I'm talking about, get the hell up, now!"

Jasper seemed so miserable, desperate for a moment, and Sofia wasn't the least tempted to fling herself into his arms and tell him anything. He was good at trying to make himself out to be the pitiful one who needed to be felt sorry for.

Chandler was such a man, with qualities more valuable than all of Earth's treasures. With Jasper, there would be worries, lies, and everything unpleasant. If she explained what happened, she knew he would not understand, and she would have at the very least no peace of mind.

She knew she could expect nothing but trouble and confusion from Jasper. Chandler, on the other hand, stood for everything that would bring her an orderly life. All the spur of the moment fun, sex in the daylight, or just getting out for the fun of it all.

Finally, she managed to mumble a few words. "I'm sorry, Jasper, but that's the way it is, and I like it this way."

"Not as sorry as I am, Sofia. Where did I go wrong? Where did we go wrong? Tell me, please," he begged. "What could I have possibly done for you to treat me this way?"

"You haven't done anything, Jasper. You had nothing to do with this," she urged.

"It was that sudden, you never even warned me this was a possibility," he went on, as though he hadn't heard a word Sofia was saying. "Couldn't we have talked this over, maybe try to work it out? Surely we can talk about it with some sort of understanding? You know all I've ever wanted is you and to see you the happiest person in the world. If only you could have thrown me a bone or something, I would have gone on that trip with you." He hesitated. "How long have you been seeing this guy without telling me?"

"I have told you over and over and over, Jasper. You weren't listening, and I'm done. You not listening to me is your problem, not mine. I got tired of talking. If you don't believe me, ask my mother. She'll tell you. You do this to yourself, and it's time for you to be going."

"So, you decide to run away to Nice and marry a man you've only known a couple of days? Especially when you told me that you would give me your answer when you got back. I believed you. I was even sure that you might have a change of mind and heart and decide to marry me. It seemed to me you were happy when we are together."

"This is your answer, and no, once again you aren't listening, Jasper. You never did, and never will. Don't you think that's why Lisa, Tammy, and Lynn did you the same way?" She added in haste, "Oh, Jasper, I'm sorry. I'm so sorry I have hurt you in any way. Sound familiar, Jasper? Now, you need to leave, and don't come back here. I gathered your things and sent them to your mother's house with Chandler."

"You sent my things back by *him*?" He looked at her with his mouth agape, frozen.

"Go. Goodbye, Jasper." He was rubbing his hands nervously. There was little about him now that could be considered attractive. "Do you really want me to answer that? Yes! I sent your things by Chandler." Sofia stared at Jasper, still sitting on the edge of her wet chair. Never once did he make the effort to take off his sloppy wet coat that was staining the chair's upholstery.

Sofia thought of Chandler—easygoing, unconcerned, with his quick wit and bright, mischievous eyes. He might not take thinking seriously, perhaps he was even too honest for his own good, but everything sprang to life when he was around. Even his arrogance and sarcasm seemed somehow precious now. And as for the sex, it was the best sex she'd ever had. Then along came Jasper, a complete opposite from Chandler. Jasper, the man sitting on her chair, looking sheepishly at her, wasn't any match for the happy-go-lucky Chandler, who lived life to its fullest.

"I'm really sorry if I've hurt you, Jasper," she murmured finally, not knowing what else to say. Tears threatened to spill, but she wiped them away quickly by looking towards the window.

"I didn't come here looking for your apologies, Sofia. I'm here because I want to try to understand. You have no reason to be sorry, and I have no intention of blaming you for anything. I love you too much for that. I love you more than you'll ever know, and I'm afraid that you may have made a terrible mistake. What was there about this man that you found so fascinating? His fortune?"

"That was a low blow, below the belt, Jasper. Don't you think so?" she said angrily. "Besides, he has no money."

"Then he must be good for something. To tell you the truth, Sofia, I don't want to meet this guy. It would be too painful for me to see the two of you together. Besides, I'm liable to bash his head in really good," Jasper said, with his beady little eyes staring at her. "When Madame Taxon told me he was in, I waited in the street, hoping he would leave. I've been walking up and down in front of the building for hours."

"I never intended to introduce you two. It's my life, Jasper, and no one says I have to obey anyone." Sofia hushed then quickly she said, "Were you in the rain all that time?"

"The rain didn't bother me. When I saw a dark-haired man leave, I knew it was him. He fitted the description Monsieur Parlay had given."

Sofia felt very uncomfortable now. "What were you doing asking my boss what was going on? That, you had and have no right to doing. I'm speaking with Ireland. She had no damn right saying or telling anyone anything." Sofia was pissed so badly that she nearly thought she was having a heart attack. She had it all bottled up for her landlady. It had been coming for a while now. She thought of the shame and grief she might have caused.

His words were the most absolutely shocking she had ever heard him speak. Her mouth fell open and she stared at him in horror. She knew she had to face each new day as it came, and without Jasper in it.

"Well, I have to admit he's better looking than I am. "He's taller, for one thing, and better dressed. In fact, I guess you could say he was an elegant man, but there are other things to consider. Tell me, Sofia, were you attracted to him just because of his looks?"

Chandler was impeccably groomed, in fact, so handsome he made Sofia feel weak just looking at him.

"You are pathetic, Jasper. Snooping into my private life when you have no right to. And besides, what kind of question is that? Marry the man because of his looks? Marry the man because he has money? Are you crazy?" She snapped hatefully, "I'm done with you, Jasper. Get it through your head!" The more he stood in front of her the more she was feeling like picking up her umbrella and hitting him over the head with it.

"Does he have a better job than me?"

"What's the point of all these questions? It is what it is, and I want you out." This was a side of Jasper she'd never seen before.

"I'm asking because I have to try to understand. I want to know you're going to be happy. That's the only way I'll ever be able to accept what you've done. If you could only realize how much this is hurting me, Sofia. I had you *way up there* on a pedestal. I wanted you to be my wife one day. You're the love of my life! I loved you so much, and I still love you. I guess I always will." He hid his face to hide away his tears with his hands.

"What have I done?" He leaned in toward her, and peered intently at her face. His gaze raked over her, and his voice deepened.

"Jasper, get out, now before I call the police. Now!" she yelled and rushed him to the door. "Get out!" She opened the door for him and gestured for him to leave. "You'll find another girl and treat her the same way."

He quickly lifted his head. "You will end up getting a divorce!"

"If I do, you will not be there to pick me up. I'll marry someone else just to get away from you if I have to."

"Have you gone mad? Sofia, what has happened to your principles? What about your religion? You know very well where my convictions lie. I could never marry a divorced woman, not even you!" He sighed heavily.

Sofia only looked at him in some confusion. Yes, it was true, but she felt a new strength was forming inside her. "You have outdone yourself this time, Jasper."

"The Lathans of the world never married divorcees." He went on, speaking vehemently. "My mother would die of shame. It would break her heart. No, no. Stay with your husband, Sofia. What's done is done, and there is no way to change it. You married that man, so you must love him. Forgive me for coming here. I shouldn't have. I see now I should have stayed away. I don't know what I expected. I'm the one who should be asking your forgiveness, because my coming here has upset you. Oh, what's the use? All I ask is that you try to avoid me at work. It shouldn't be too difficult. Our offices aren't close together, and there won't be any reason for us to see each other. I wish you nothing but the best, and I hope your marriage is a very happy one."

With no further explanation he made wide strides to the doorway. Standing in the doorway, he turned one last time to look at Sofia. His eyes were filled with despair. "Where my mind is, lost! But I'm getting both back, because I can't live this way!" He stormed out swearing, and for a moment Sofia was stunned. He turned for the stairs, where the elevator door stood open.

Sofia reached out to touch his arm. She wanted to shove him down the elevator shaft. She caught control of her anger. She would hate him forever.

With his back to her, he was silent a moment, then said, "It's over, Sofia. I will be no bother to you any longer."

Sofia stood motionless. Inside her apartment, she crumpled against the door and began to weep openly, clasping her face, her cheeks soon wet with tears. How horrible to hurt anyone. Certainly, Jasper didn't deserve to be treated this way, and now that he had left, Sofia's last chance to straighten out the situation had left with him. Suddenly she felt quite alone and helpless, much like a castaway adrift on a raft in the middle of an unfriendly ocean. She watched until he disappeared into the shadows. After a timeless battle of fighting tears, she roused her thoughts to Chandler.

Then she realized how odd she must look. Sofia made her way back to the sofa and plopped down. Unable to conceal her emotions, she propped herself up on her elbows, held her head and wept aloud. *If only the clock could be turned back, if only it could.* Already the thought was splicing through her mind. *How different life could have been—would have been.*

Finally she raised her head and wiped away the tears, to return to her book. Then suddenly she remembered her chair. It was soaking wet from Jasper's damn coat. He had just hurled himself in it, not caring at all that he was wet.

In the next moment, she burst into tears again, her happiness mixed with a strange feeling of relief. For a long time, she continued to weep.

It became painful for Sofia. She was right—Jasper had lied to her. She had allowed herself to open up to the bastard, and look what had happened. It would not happen a second time. If he showed his face around here again, she would put him out and put all the blame on him, making her look the pitiful one.

She felt Chandler's departure deeper than she had ever felt anything. Her mind continuously wandered over the time they had shared. She couldn't eat or sleep. How could she do such a thing? It didn't matter what direction she went—nothing was working nor helping.

One should never marry a man out of pity. Jasper, with all his bad qualities, would surely be a perfect husband for the right woman. But not Sofia, and she couldn't help but wonder why, suddenly, she had begun to expect so much more out of life. Why was she no longer able to be content with a man such as Jasper? And why did she suddenly feel this great capacity for love within herself, the kind of love that would blossom, make her feel like a woman, the kind of love that required someone worthwhile to receive it?

What forces were being unleashed within her? What if she never found the man who would bring out all the love she was sure she had to give? Then she would be left a lonely woman, to live only with regrets.

Her mind was flooded with confusion. Did she think she owed him? Her mind, her actions, were so radically different from any Jasper had ever known. Sofia had changed, and her feelings were now for another man.

Wasn't it better to have someone, even if that someone wasn't able to make her feel that special way, than no one at all? More than likely, Chandler would soon disappear from her life forever. And when that happened, what would she do?

Oh, why couldn't her heart be more reasonable? Why had it suddenly become so difficult to be sensible?

The following day, Sofia had something else to worry about.

Sofia roused from sleep slowly. Chandler was in the room again, and she stirred under the down quilt and smiled a little to herself. She blinked sleepily, moving a hand toward his pillow, then sat up with a start. It was almost dawn. The sky was light, and the starts were gone. Her gaze flew to the door, and there stood Chandler, slumped against the sill, staring at her.

Sofia whirled and strode to the side of the bed to grab her robe.

"Chandler," Sofia said, "I have got to speak to you. Are you just now noticing your ass never came back last night, and I'm not answering to anyone for it. I don't care who you were laid up with, but you have caused me more trouble than you're worth. I'm done with this shit and I want you to go!" She paused for a quick breath. "It's for the best that you just get your things and don't look back. I can't do this any longer." The longer she stood staring at Chandler, the more upset she became.

"I know you are upset with me, darling. Are you trying to find a way to tell me I'm not the ideal tenant you thought me to be?"

"What the hell—what is it with men? You are all a bunch of dumbasses. I don't know who's deafer, you or Jasper. No, yes, no, oh I know, I was right the first time." Sofia was so angry she felt as if her head was splitting down the middle. "I'll pack your effects and you can leave, now!"

His lack of response drew her courage further out. It was rare that she had a chance to spew her anger and sarcasm without fear of retribution.

Chandler looked at Sofia in silence for a moment. "I have an explanation."

She took in a deep breath, "I'm not interested in your explanation. I've got to figure something out for Saturday." Sofia took giant strides across the room to avoid being near Chandler. She knew where it would lead if she got the slightest bit close to him. She bent her head to keep from looking at him. "You've known all along about the little agreement we have, and you just take it upon yourself to make me look like a fool. I'm no fool and I'm not taking it any more. You need to leave and take your things with you."

"No, I'm not. I have an explanation, and I'm telling you." He held up one finger and was looking at the loveliness of her face. Her lips were beautifully formed and naturally deep velvet red. Jet black lashes long and thick, they looked almost real. Now, he felt a sudden shortness of breath, a strange feeling flooding him. He was finding it hard not to just take her within his arms and make passionate love to her. He had never played second fiddle to any man and he wasn't about to start now, if that damn Jasper had something to do with this.

"Fine. I can't stop you, anyway." Sofia stopped for a fraction of a second, her features ridiculous. She stepped back from him Apparently suddenly self-conscious, she crossed her arms across her breasts and watched him intently. Her eyes widened, she gave a quick shake of her head. A small snide smile twisted her lips as she gazed at his face.

"I was at the casino. I had no money and thought I could get my hands on some at the craps tables. I was on them all night." He bent his head in disgrace. He was in a time of need.

"The casino!" Sofia shouted out loud.

"I have my ticket if you don't believe that. You can go see the waiter. I felt so bad about taking your money that I had to do something. That's where I got the money I left on the countertop in the kitchen." He took a big breath and started to say something, but didn't. "It's sort of a pride thing we men have."

"I can't believe this." With an infuriated groan, she spun around and located her chair.

"Look, I know where I was and I can prove it. Either let it go, or I'll get my things and leave." He hesitated. "I'm a living, breathing human being, and I do have some pride." He took several steps across the room towards the bedroom to retrieve his effects.

"Stop. I'm sorry you felt like you had to go to the casino for money. You don't have to do that. I just wished you would have called, or at least been honest with me about it if you needed money."

"So, we are on for the boss's party on Saturday?" He smiled happily.

"Of course. You'll probably be bored to death. Madame Parlay will be there, with their two daughters, their husbands, and their children. A typical family dinner, and they are simple people. I know they aren't your kind. You may not find it easy to fit in with them."

"Don't you worry your pretty little head about that. I can adapt myself to any kind of situation and I can get along with all types of people, and besides, I love children."

"They think of you as my husband and are anxious to meet you, so I hope you won't make fun of them. They're a very nice family and everyone loves them. And you can be impossibly arrogant at times."

"Really," he said, arching his eyebrows. "It must be an overreaction to your worrying so much about me and what's going to happen next. But this time you can relax. I'll behave like an angel . . . that is, unless you would like me to show some of that mental cruelty you'll be using to get our divorce."

"Oh, don't you dare, Chandler! Stop poking fun at me."

"Fine, mental cruelty is out. But maybe there should be a little restlessness, some small display of discontent, perhaps, with being your husband."

"Just don't overdo it, okay?"

"Fair enough. Not too much, not too little. That suits me fine. Just leave it to me." For an instant Chandler stood in silence, looking at her innocent, beautiful face. Then slowly he shook his head.

Finally he took a step toward his room, then stopped and turned around. "Black tie?"

"No. Just wear your most sober suit."

"Got it. I will follow your instructions to the letter, so you can stop worrying. Goodnight, boss."

Chandler stepped out toward his room and Sofia to hers. But she couldn't relax. She didn't trust Chandler and didn't quite know what to expect. One thing was for sure—and that was he knew his way around a woman's body.

CHAPTER FIVE

The next evening, suddenly Sofia felt Chandler's presence very close to her. She felt his chest against her back.

"You are so beautiful," he whispered tenderly, his breath caressing her hair, her ear. "I want to kiss you, if you will allow me to."

As she turned slowly, her eyes once again bright in the light's reflection. "I want you to," she whispered back to him.

He reached out, touching her cheek, his fingertips drawing her to him. He pressed his warm, moist lips lightly at the corner of her mouth. Then he pulled away slightly and sighed. He took her chin in one hand and lifted her face to his. "Sofia," he said softly as magnetic blue lights danced in his irises, "most women in today's world would object to being totally dominated by a man. You've been very sheltered, and I want to know that you are mine. Like right now, if I wanted to take advantage of you, would you try to stop me?"

Never had she been so conscious of a face, never so fascinated with anyone as with the tall man touching her chin. Her lips parted as she titled her head slightly to one side. A whirlwind of emotions tore at her heart. Then she gave him a slow bewitching smile. "I won't stop you," she whispered. "Unless you prefer it that way."

He started to speak but faltered. His eyes were on fire, and the glare of that heat consumed his face. Slowly he bent forward and placed his mouth directly on hers.

She felt the quiver of his lips throughout her body, felt the warmth of his hands, his fingers pressing into her back. She was totally unprepared for the roaring in her head, the strange, off-balance sensation gripping her, as though some invisible breeze were swaying her. She couldn't stop the blood from raging, and for a moment she felt almost frightened by the intensity of her feelings. Hardly able to breathe, she pulled her mouth from his and gasped aloud, and at hearing the sound escape her mouth, immediately dipped her head.

"What is it?" he murmured softly.

"I—I don't know." Her words were weak. "I feel—strange." Her throat was so numb, she could hardly swallow.

A knowing glint appeared in Chandler's eyes. "Are you okay?" he asked gently, searching her face.

"I think so." She felt him softly brush her cheek with one of his hands, then his mouth again found her lips, softly at first, changing to an aggressive forcefulness. She blazed as if she had been burned. She felt his strength, the power of his arms around her, and in a moment, she knew it could never stop. She kissed his lips in a way she had never dreamed—freely, blissfully.

She slipped her arms around his neck, easing her fingers into his hair with such a delicate movement she was hardly aware of their actions. Held tight in his arms, she felt his embrace mold her body to his. Her hunger grew. In the heat of desire his mouth plundered hers and his tongue reached for hers.

Then the long embrace was broken. Stepping back, he placed his hands at the buttons of her blouse. She held her breath, feeling as if she were floating on the brink of some wonderful discovery. He ripped the blouse open, buttons popping and flying in disarray, and a low moan escaped from deep within his throat.

The hot wetness of his lips brushing over hers brought such pleasure, she wanted it aggressive. With a soft cry she twisted her body away so that she stood free of him, shivering, eyeing him through a veil of delirium.

He leaned very close to her and considered her face. The tip of her tongue emerged between her white teeth and she caught it in a little bite as her eyes fastened unblinkingly to his. "Sofia," he said in a thick voice that seemed to come from far away. "You are so beautiful. I want you, now, here." In a flowing motion his hand twined in her hair, boldly stroking her breasts, his fingers hard against her flesh, pressing, taunting her nipples.

Her face was flushed, and her mouth was dry. The thought crossed her mind that she breathed like this when she had run a 5K run. She was ready for him and wanted all he had to offer.

"Take me," she whispered demandingly. Her gaze followed his hands as he unbuttoned his shirt and pulled it off, leaving him naked from the waist up. It was the first time she had looked closely at his chest. She became totally absorbed as he reached for his pants. Nothing could break her concentration now.

That was all it took. Chandler turned in an instant. He unfastened her jeans and pulled them down in one sweep, lifted her to his hips and carried her to the bed. Her hands caught as she fell across it. This time she didn't close her eyes nor change her expression.

He drew back and whispered, "You are now mine . . .you are *mine.*"

Not looking at all nervous, he stripped to form-fitting briefs and she looked down, then up to his face with searching eyes.

He looked at her through half-closed eyes. Before she

could move, he leaned his upper body forward and pressed his mouth to hers, and she felt the naked hunger in his kiss.

When he pressed the entire length of his body against hers, he found her softness and then suddenly, he flipped her on her knees. He wanted to be deep inside her. It was a dangerous and controlling desire. He reached for her hair, tilting her head back as he made his way inside, forcing her to take him. It brought her to orgasm right away and he could feel her.

"Don't stop, don't stop!" she whispered. This time she closed her eyes and all the muscles in her body tightened. The kiss extended into another, each one more severe, harsh, more probing. She urged him on for more, and harder.

"How does that feel? You want it harder?" he demanded when he jerked her head up to him. He leaned to her, licking her neck and to her ear. "Tell me!" he whispered.

"Yes, fuck me," she replied as she was out of breath. She was starting to perspire, her hair damp from behind.

"You like it?"

"I like it, I like it!" she replied, out of breath.

"You like it when I fuck you this way?" He hesitated. "Answer me," he demanded.

"Yes, I like it." She hesitated. "Fuck me, hard!"

The more she said to him, the harder it was for him to keep from ending the show too soon. She'd never felt anything like it—he was huge, and the more she talked to him, the more dominating he was. He got off on it. He had to stop in mid-stream several times to keep from coming too soon.

But the last time was too late, he couldn't hold back any longer. He pulled out and jacked off on her ass. He, too, could be versatile.

"I need a shower," Sofia puffed. "What about you?"

"Ah, I think I need one, also," he replied, out of breath and unable to move. "I'll wait until you get done. I can't move right now."

As it turned out, Sofia's fears were groundless. The dinner was a huge success. And Chandler, in large part, was responsible.

He was likable and jovial, apparently supremely happy with the way things were going. He complimented the cook, praised Parlay's home, listened respectfully to Parlay's endless stories, displayed great interest in the young married couples, and completely enchanted the children.

As it came time to withdraw to the living room, Chandler had taken two of the kids on his knees and seemed to be delighted as they tugged at his tie and pulled his hair.

Sofia couldn't remember ever having such a good time at the Parlay's. She had always been in awe of her boss and his family, and as a result most of the conversation had dealt either with inflation or the problems of the blue-collar workers. Without trying to impress anyone or take over the conversation, Chandler had kept the evening light and easy with amusing anecdotes about things that happened to him on his travels. Everyone was lighthearted with a great deal of laughter throughout the room. It had been very much unlike Sofia's other dinners at the Parlays, when she had been accompanied by Jasper and his mother. This time, there had been only one point where Sofia felt slightly embarrassed. Parlay had asked Chandler a question about his work. To her knowledge, he had no regular employment and spent most of his days in his room, apparently idle.

Chandler had answered nonchalantly, "Well, you know, good jobs and decent salaries are fairly easy to come by at Goldbond."

Sofia sighed with relief. Chandler always seemed able to extricate himself from a tight situation with a vague remark. It was true that there were many high-paying and interesting positions at Goldbond, the second largest manufacturing plant in France, and Chandler hadn't lied.

When it was time for them to leave, a very impressed Parlay whispered in Sofia's ear *how lucky she was to have a husband like Chandler*. He told her that they could well understand now why she had married him and how happy they were with her choice.

Sofia expected to take the subway back to her apartment, but Chandler, apparently very pleased with himself, flagged a taxi. He smiled as he opened the door for Sofia to get in first—a fine gentleman he was, as the English generally were.

Sofia rolled the window down on her side, and the breeze blew her hair across her face, which she didn't even bother to push away. Elbow propped on the door, she drummed out the beat of the song playing on the radio. Even a routine drive gave Sofia a sense of exhilaration and an appreciation of Chandler's upbeat pace. Cars darted from lane to lane, and men hung recklessly to the sides of trucks, as if life for them was one giant, fun fair.

"You should wear red more often," Chandler said suddenly.

Sofia turned to him, a flutter of pleasure rippling through her. She had not even been aware he'd noticed her dress. "Thank you. Red's one of my favorite colors, aside from pastels, of course. I seldom have the nerve to wear it." She looked down at the silk dress. It had a wide neckline that could slip over one shoulder. She enjoyed wearing it, when she did. She felt casual, comfortable . . . and a little daring.

"Why are you afraid to wear your favorite color?"

"I don't really know," Sofia admitted, grateful for the darkness that hid her embarrassment. Why couldn't she have kept her mouth shut? "I don't wear clothes that distract from my . . . well, professional image."

"That's nonsense—you are beautiful and should act that

way."

"I hope you weren't too bored."

"Not at all. In fact, quite the contrary, to answer your question. They are wonderful people, your friends. I love to be around people like the Parlays. I don't meet too many in my surroundings and I find it refreshing when I do."

Sofia felt herself reacting in a somber way to what he said. What kind of people did he hang with? Not wanting to pry, she simply went on with the conversation, thinking he didn't notice her behavior.

"I couldn't help but notice how you were with their children."

"I adore children. I could play with them for hours. What do you think I am, Sofia? An ogre?" He asked the question with one brow raised as he stared at her eye to eye, as if he was trying to pull something out of her.

"No, but you are different, very different when you're with me, and I can't help wonder what you're like when I'm not around," she replied.

"That's because I'm usually on the defensive with you."

"On the defensive with me?" she repeated hastily.

"Yes. If I were to allow myself . . . you are young, Sofia, and so naïve. Yet you're fascinating to be around. When we were having dinner, I watched you. You were the most beautiful woman there, and the most pleasant, I might add. I was proud of you, proud to be with you. You were almost," he hesitated, "but we have an agreement, don't we? And I don't think it would be right for me to go on. It would only annoy you."

Sofia still didn't understand what he was talking about. Quietly, he took her hand in both of his and pressed it gently, holding with one, kissing with the other. "Please forgive me, if you will, my sweet Sofia. Sometimes I seem a bit harsh or brutal with you. Believe me, it's only because I feel it's for the best."

They emerged from the countryside, and Chandler looked her over when they stopped at the traffic light. The taxi was pulling up in front of the apartment building, and Sofia didn't have a chance to ask why. She tucked the question away, so as not to forget to ask as soon as they were inside her apartment.

Chandler paid the driver and offered his hand.

Seeing the sparkle in his eyes, she emerged from the cab, gladly taking the hand he offered. She was flattered that his temptations were behaving.

Once they were in the apartment, Sofia was in much better humor. She still looked tired, but the lines of tension on her brow had eased, and she seemed much more relaxed.

"After such a beautiful evening, don't you think it would be a shame for us just to say goodnight and go to our separate rooms?"

Sofia's face lit up with joy. "Oh, yes! I have a great chilled white wine. I can't help but love the stuff. I'll go and get the glasses. Wait for me in the living room."

When she got back, Chandler was examining the room. "This is a very lovely apartment. You've decorated it tastefully. It's bright and intimate. Guess I've never really noticed until now. Ah! I see you have quite a collection of books."

Chandler had turned around and was gazing at the books as though he had suddenly discovered a bunch of old friends.

"Do you like to read, Chandler?"

"I do, very much. When they are well-chosen, books can make life so much more enjoyable. And when you have books, you are never alone."

It was obvious that the very sight of certain titles made him happy. Seeing his reaction, Sofia realized there was a side of this man that was refined, intelligent and quite intellectual. Under the unconcerned and carefree attitude was another Chandler, much more serious and to Sofia, much more interesting.

Total silence descended for a moment, then she said calmly, "Yeah, I have one author that I absolutely love his work. I make sure to have every novel he writes."

"I see you have quite a range here—some serious, some not too serious," he continued. "Three novels by Stenberg. How about that," he finished, amusement in his tone.

"Why not? Don't you think I have the brain to understand them?"

"Of course I do! I'm just glad to see that you like him, too."

"Not only do I like him, I believe he's one of the few authors who puts into words those vague feelings and reactions so few are able to express. I found myself buried in the character of Borge, with all her hopes. In Abby, with her shyness. You'll probably think I'm crazy, but sometimes when I'm reading Stenberg I feel there's a very strong connection between us."

"There's nothing strange about that. On the contrary, your enthusiasm for him makes me happy. May I?" He took one of the books from the shelf and opened it. "In English, too."

"I studied English for my degree. I can read it quite well, but I have problems trying to speak it."

"Did you read the jacket?"

"Of course. He sounds like quite an author, don't you agree? Do you know the author?"

Without answering, Chandler was reading the bio of her author. *Born in London, Stenberg was a brilliant student at Oxford. The incredible success of his first novel convinced him to become a full-time writer. A world traveler, Stenberg is a man very concerned about world issues. He has a great writing style, humor and a depth of thought that places him in the unique position of being able to be appreciated by everyone. He ranks high among the great English authors of modern times.*

"Not bad," Chandler said, looking to make sure the book was placed back in its original space so that Sofia wouldn't have any difficulties locating it when she wanted.

"Yes, I think Stenberg is a remarkable writer. I wish the publishers had put his picture on the back cover. I really would like to know what he looks like."

Chandler quickly spun around to face Sofia. "What do you think he looks like?"

"Oh, I see him as a man in his forties, with brown hair and intelligent eyes. He is probably quite intimidating, yet humorous at times, too, don't you think? And I love English humor. Somehow, it doesn't seem to be heavy or vulgar."

It was late, and a tiring day. They parted with a warm hug. Sofia went to her bedroom door and opened it slowly. Her heart seemed to rise in her throat as she stood at the doorway, transfixed with a sudden desire to be with Chandler.

It was a beautiful evening, cool and brisk, with small white puffs of clouds drifting across a brilliant starry sky. Under the full moon the great live oaks with their hanging moss seemed to stand like grey sentinels. The air hung still and quiet, no breeze stirring, and a small night sounds drifted up to the window. A few lights from across the street with an occasional voice drifting up.

"My first night was a night to remember, Sofia. I never want it to change." Chandler took it one step further. He wasn't about to let her go without saying goodnight without a proper kiss. He could feel his strange possessiveness towards Sofia. His eyes gleamed as he stared at her.

Sofia returned a warm, friendly smile, her cheeks pinkening. Her eyes raised slowly to meet his gaze, she swallowed hard and turned her full attention to him. Her face swam in a vision before him with eyes dark and sultry, and a small tongue darting about moist lips.

Her hair seemed to beckon him closer and caress her as he kissed her. Her arms were open and welcoming, and her fingers caressed him as his hands found her sensuous breasts and titillated them to excited peaks. He looked at her, bare and flowing, golden in the soft light. His eyes went over her slowly in a longing manner, to caress her figure of silken flesh. All his senses were completely occupied with her.

Gazing down, he saw her as innocent and tender. she was from a different mold which he had never known. His mind was filled with the feel of her warm and soft against him, her tender breasts for him to have only. His manhood rose as he wanted to take her, with force, the way she liked it. His raging desire overcame his common sense and he grasped her roughly from behind, one hand crushing a tempting breast while the other slid downward over her belly to rest between her thighs, his lips hungrily seeking her flesh. She gasped in equal parts of anger and surprise at the swiftness of his passion, then whirled, and, with all her strength, begged for more.

Time was forgotten as they lay in the darkness.

Sofia's mind heard only muddled words. With a smoldering gaze she watched him, admiring the long, sinewy muscles of his body, narrow hips and broad shoulders. She was suddenly filled with a possessive pride, knowing that he was hers and no other woman had a right to claim him.

He pressed his entry home and she arched her back and withed in ecstasy as their fervor mounted. His manhood and mind linked him to her.

When a gentle breeze ruffled the curtains by her bed the next morning, Sofia stirred from sleep. A dull ache in her back, she felt strangely tired. With a yawn she knew the reason—Chandler had his elbow in the center of her back. She was happily trapped within his arms.

They seized the opportunity to get to know one another outside the sex. Getting to know each other, Sofia had never spent that kind of time with anyone like Chandler. She wouldn't have it any other way. It was the perfect beginning to the day.

CHAPTER SIX

"Sofia," he called out, "I've just rented a car for my stay in Paris. Would you like to drive to the country and have breakfast at one of those romantic inns with me on Sunday?" He was like a child with a new toy.

Sofia didn't take the time to stop to wonder how someone without any money could afford to rent a car. She was quick to answer. "Of course! It's awfully nice of you to do this. It's not every day a girl gets an offer for a ride in the county."

"Sometimes, I get the feeling that you want to avoid me, and I must admit, I don't much like that feeling. Besides, your being indoors all the time isn't good for your health. You need some fresh air and sunshine. And you might as well know that I almost never do anything I don't want to do. So, you'll come?"

"I wouldn't miss it for the world!" She smiled. "I've not been asked to go for a ride in the country in such a long while." A drive in the country would be nice.

It was much more than that, and she was looking so forward to getting out of the city for a while. The weatherman was calling for a beautiful Sunday.

The next few days went by slowly at first, then out of the blue they started to fly by. Worrying of what to wear, and how to look? These things concerned her, because she wanted to keep the spark they had together.

The closer Sunday got, the more it became real to her. She was in a relationship she had never forecast for her future. They were acting like a couple—going out, being seen in town, eating at nice restaurants, going on outings, going on adventures—a true relationship, but it wasn't a true relationship. She could opt out anytime she wanted.

Sunday arrived, and Sofia chose to wear a nice dress with a cute pair of sandals, and her hair pinned up. It was to be a fantastic afternoon. Sofia was hungry, as was Chandler. Apparently, he knew where he was going, because he drove straight there. The inn was filled with laughing, chattering people of all sorts. An old country estate had been converted to a bed-n-breakfast, with many verandas and terraces, and the food was served in the open air. The patrons sat at wrought-iron tables with fresh flowers for centerpieces accenting the décor.

"What a charming place." Sofia smiled. "Listen to the birds singing. It's so wonderful to sit in the shade of these lovely old trees and have breakfast. I've never been here before, I have to admit," Sofia admitted shyly. "You are right about me not getting out more, and I see clearly what I'm missing by staying cooped up in my apartment." She was bubbling with joy, and as he looked at her, Chandler's face showed great affection.

"It's nice to see you smile, Sofia. You are living like a hermit, if you don't mind me saying. It's time you realized you're a young woman needing to express herself to the world. You should be going out, shopping, pampering yourself, and you are in a small apartment with a nine to five job."

Radiantly lovely in her white dress, Sofia looked at Chandler with all the gratitude she felt shining in her eyes.

Elegant, as usual, he was dressed in a pair of jeans, which were pressed to perfection, a brown jacket, and a soft, yellow cotton shirt. Everything he was wearing looked to be expensive. But again, where did he get such fine things with no money?

Chandler was attentive, and Sofia couldn't imagine a more enjoyable companion to spend her afternoon with. His conversations were light, but interesting, captivating Sofia's attention. She realized he was a man of considerable culture and education, and she was fascinated by his ability to leave behind all his usual foolishness.

Just knowing that Chandler was part of these marvelous hours made everything perfect. After lunch on the sidewalk, they decided to take a romantic drive through the country-side. There was a beautiful park Sofia really enjoyed. Chandler stopped the car so they could walk through and admire the serene setting surrounding Paris. Sofia felt almost euphoric. The fresh air and sunshine, as well as her special happiness, brought new color to her cheeks. She was like a carefree little girl again, enchanted by the beauties of nature, letting the wind caress her face.

"What an incredible day, Chandler," Sofia smiled. "Thank you. I didn't think I've ever enjoyed myself so much. And to think it was right here in my own back yard. People travel thousands of miles just to experience a day such as ours."

The inn wasn't exactly cheap. Sofia felt it would have been proper for him to allow her to share in the expense. As they headed back to Paris, a little of the intoxication was beginning to wear off. She found herself coming back down to earth, and began to worry about how much this must have cost Chandler. She didn't pay for anything. Even though she had offered to share the expenses, he had flatly refused.

He was being generous with her. Generosity took money, and he wasn't living on credit, that much she was sure of.

Now it was weighing on her mind—if only he would spend all day in the apartment, instead of dreaming and wasting precious time. Chandler went out only for breakfast and lunch, and in the evening, he would leave—for where? She didn't know, but she was sure that wherever he went, it must be nice. How could he afford so much if he was out of work? Something was fishy about her handsome husband, and she aimed to find out.

Looking at his finely sculptured profile, admiring the assurance with which he handled the car, Sofia decided to come right out with what was bothering her.

"When do you think you'll be starting work, Chandler?" she asked.

Chandler glanced at her, his face reflecting amusement. "What do you mean by work?"

"It's a thing called a job. No one can get by for very long at a time without money unless, of course, one has a fortune to depend on." Sofia was digging, but she was no writer and her intentions didn't fall on deaf shoulders.

"Well, that certainly doesn't apply to me."

"But surely there must be something you can do. Your money will run out soon. I don't know what you have and it's none of my business. I just know that it will only go so far. Besides, what type of work have you done? What do you do best?"

"Oh, a lot of things. I'm very good at being sociable. I play a good game of golf, I drive a car very well. And . . . I'm gentle with women, and when it's required, I can be a very good husband."

"That's not an answer, Chandler."

"No? Sorry about that." He gave her a charming smile. "I intrigue you, don't I?"

"Too much, sometimes. Chandler, it isn't good to lie around all day doing nothing. You know the old saying *The devil finds work for idle hands*?" She hesitated briefly, "I have to work to keep these high standards around here." The merchants around town had refused her credit and she worked it all out herself.

Then, thinking she might have offended him, she quickly

added, "I don't think you're at that stage yet, at least, I hope not. If I found you a job, would you take it?" She shook her head slowly, dropping her gaze to the floor. He laughed softly and came towards her.

"Why not? I will take the job. I love trying new things. There really isn't much I can't do. So, what did you have in mind?" He laughed gently and made a sweeping bow.

"Now, I'm not sure. Not something at the Parlay plant, that's for sure. Not only would it confuse Parlay, but it would be very awkward for you to be working at the same place as Jasper. I meet a lot of people from other businesses. Let me see if one of them has an opening."

"Go right ahead. The road is all clear. I don't mind working with this Jasper fellow. If I can work with him, then it's nothing to any of the others." Chandler agreed, he didn't have a care in the world, or at least that's how Sofia took it.

"Does this make you happy?"

"Very!" Sofia smiled. *He's going to work whether he likes it or not.*

He moved closer, and in a rapid movement, slipped his arm about her waist, nearly lifting her from the floor, and then covered her mouth with his, engulfing Sofia in a heady scent, not unlike that of a brandy she had, tucked away for special occasions. She was too surprised to resist and hung limp in his embrace. She saw herself as if from outside her body and, mildly amused, felt his tongue parting her lips and thrusting within. From a low level of consciousness grew a pleasure like no other.

A few days passed, and Chandler asked her if she had learned of anything opening for him to pursue.

"Nothing yet, or at least anything that would suit you."

"What do you mean—suit me, or be too good?"

"You're insane. What does that matter, as long as it's a

job?" she replied with a nod.

"It doesn't."

"Are you getting snippy with me, or did I take that the wrong way?" Sofia asked politely.

"Of course not. What's the job?"

"Well, somehow I can't see you wrapping parcels in a basement just a few hours a week." Her mind stopped and held for a moment.

"Why not? I think that's marvelous. Sometimes I feel like I was born to wrap parcels in a basement. What does it pay?"

"Fifteen hundred."

A frown wrinkled his brows. "Per week?"

"Per month," she replied. "Have you never worked a regular job, Chandler?" Oh, Lord, she thought, he's never worked a public job.

"I don't think so. Depends on what you call a regular job."

"Chandler!"

"Not at all. I've done a lot of things in my life, but I've never wrapped parcels in a basement. I told you before, I love new challenges." His eyes centered on her. "I won't fail you, I promise."

"You'll be working with ordinary people, you know."

"The more ordinary the better, I say. Ordinary people fascinate me. Give me the address and hope that the job is still open by the time I get there."

Sofia could scarcely believe her ears.

She was even more incredulous when Chandler came back and told her he had been hired.

For days, Chandler left the apartment very early and didn't get back until late at night.

"It's absolutely incredible," Chandler kept saying. He seemed to be faithful to his new job, but for some reason Sofia had her doubts. Was he really going to work every day? How was he getting along? She knew where he was working and decided to pay him a visit.

No one questioned her when she went in, and as she approached the basement area, she could hear singing and Chandler's voice above the others, "All together now, for the chorus."

Sofia pushed the door open and stood observing in the doorway. The place was buzzing with activity. Some people were dining and other were nursing their drinks while engaged in highly animated discussions. Looking radiant, sure enough, there stood Chandler, surrounded by piles of paper, string, and cardboard, singing at the top of his lungs.

"Pay attention, Emily, you're missing the beat!" he shouted, laughing.

All the girls were enthralled, and the one he had called Emily was gazing at him adoringly. The singing started again, and with more enthusiasm than before, everyone returned to their wrapping, working together to the tempo of the song. Sofia turned and left without a word. Now she understood everything.

"Now you can give me any size parcels you need wrapped, because I am the best wrapper in town. I've become quite the expert."

Two days later, Chandler was fired. A grouchy inspector, he explained, came flying through the door.

"Sofia," he yelled. "That boss of yours insisted I was disrupting everything and slowing down the production line by singing while I was wrapping parcels in a basement. Just the same, it was a lot of fun and those darling girls cried when he ran me off. Emily, especially, didn't want me to leave." He stopped suddenly and looked at Sofia, standing staring at him. "Why are you frowning at me, Sofia? I thought it was cute of her to do that when I left."

"Imagine that, Chandler. For Emily, she gets near you one more time and I'll show her what taking up for another woman's husband is really like." Why did she just say that? Her secret was revealed, now he knew she loved him. It spewed from her lips, not exactly the right way, but the point made it through.

Chandler brushed her hair from her brow with his fingers. "You gave my heart a start," he laughed.

"I'm sorry," she murmured. "I didn't mean to blow up like that." She was trembling, conscious of Chandler's searing gaze upon her.

The phone rang the next morning. "Oh, the ID says it's your Aunt Lilly." Chandler said sleepily. Sofia was laying comfortably inside his arms.

"Damn it!" she whispered lightly. "Tell her I'm in the shower or something."

"I can't, I just told her to hold on. Come on, she's your family and you shouldn't shut your family out."

Sofia considered his eyes. He was gentle, unlike anyone she'd ever known. "Hand me the phone," she smiled. "Hi, Aunt Lilly."

"Not so much as a note or even a card! If it hadn't been for Parlay, I still wouldn't know. You're a naughty niece, Sofia. I'm extremely upset with you, and I'm sure you know why. I'm so upset, in fact, that I thought it better to wait a few days before calling. How could you get married without telling me?"

"I didn't tell anyone, Aunt Lilly. It was one of those spur of the moment things, and I'm sorry for not calling you when we got back." Sofia looked harsh and rolled her eyes in Chandler's face before mocking her aunt.

"Well, that's natural, I guess, especially in young people

these days. Parlay told me what a nice young man he is, and I want to meet him. Does he have a car?"

"We have a rental for now."

"Good—it's only eight miles to my place from yours, and it doesn't take any time at all to get here. I want you both here for the weekend. I have a room all ready for you, and I hope my new nephew likes to eat. You know how much old Nanny likes to cook."

"I-I'm not sure if the whole weekend would be possible, Aunt Lilly," stammered Sofia in a panic at the idea of the *room ready for you.*

"What about Sunday then? You're free on Saturday, aren't you?"

"I am . . . but I'm afraid Chandler isn't."

"Nobody works on Saturday, Sofia."

"He's a very busy man, Aunt Lilly," insisted Sofia, thinking of the single bedroom being offered. "We'll be very happy to come for lunch on Sunday and spend the entire day with you, I promise, and thank you for asking us over, Aunt Lilly. We'll see you on Sunday. Love you!"

"I'm looking forward to meeting your Mr. Right, Sofia. Love you, my little Sofia." Her words were soft yet demanding at the same time. Sofia knew something had to be done, or she'll be sharing a bed for the wrong reasons.

She hung up, relieved, and fell back on her pillow. "Now, that was a close call," Sofia replied, with a deep sigh of relief.

Chandler had no objections to going to Sofia's aunt on Sunday.

"I go to the nine AM Mass, Chandler, so we can leave in lots of time to get there for lunch. The chapel is close by, just a few blocks away from here, in fact."

"I'd better get ready to go with you. That way I'll be able to take the car and leave from the church. There won't be any problem with parking on a Sunday morning."

She looked at him in amazement. *Who is this man?* Was she dreaming? "You're going to church with me Sunday also?"

Chandler laughed. "Did you think I was an atheist? My father was a Protestant, but my mother was a Catholic, and she raised me in her faith."

Sofia was still staring at him with disbelief.

He added, smiling, "To be honest with you, I'm not the greatest Catholic in the world, far from it, actually. I do believe in God, and I'll go to Mass with you on Sunday."

All through the service on Sunday, Sofia was impressed by Chandler's apparent piety, and as they left the church, she was struck by his serious expression. Now she was seeing yet another side of Chandler.

Coming down the steps, he took her by the arm and said, "Mass is no longer the way it was when I was a child. We went to a church where Latin was still compulsory. However, I must admit I like the community feeling one gets from the modern way. It seems that people are able to understand what it's all about. Thank you for taking me along."

"See? The car hasn't been towed away and it's a beautiful day. We're very lucky. We better get going." Sofia was extremely curious. A prayer was too personal a thing to question him about. At any rate, there wasn't time for her to ask him, because he resorted to his usual jovial banter.

Chandler started the car, and since traffic was light, they drove out of Paris very quickly. When they reached the Saint-Denis, Chandler made a detour, so they could see the old Basilica.

"Fascinating to see. The good King George, who we are told was quite absentminded come to think of it, he might not have been as hopeless as we've been led to believe. And, for your information, Blanche de Castille, Du Guesclin,

Catherine de Medicis, and many others are buried here."

"Chandler, I'm really surprised with all the things you seem to know. Most of the time you act so silly. It's bewildering."

"One thing doesn't necessarily cancel out the other, you know. We have just a little farther to go," Chandler replied. There was something else that provided further evidence he was extremely well-read.

"Forgive me, if I seem to be showing off again," he began pompously. "This is where the Chateau de la Charrette is located, the place where Madame d'Epinay used to receive Jean-Jacques Rousseau. Now, that's the kind of information I consider worth remembering."

Then his tone changed. "Now, tell me something about your aunt, so I won't go in there and make a complete fool of myself."

For a moment, Sofia looked troubled. "I'm not sure you'll take to her, Chandler. I like her because she's honest and very straightforward. But she's an old lady that is set in her ways, and she doesn't beat around the bush. She'll tell you exactly what she thinks. She led her husband around by the nose, and I think she liked it that way . . . a lot. Her husband was such a lazy character and she's always been so full of life. She still bubbles over, despite her age."

"Is she a fashionable dresser?"

"Not in the least! She wears her hair in a bun and dresses like all old women who lives in the country. There's nothing fancy about her. She considers makeup and hairdressers a complete waste of time and money. But she does love nice things and keeps her house immaculate."

"I see," said Chandler. "Does she live alone?"

"No, she still has old Nanny who has been with her since she was a child. And Nanny's husband tends the gardens. He loves to be out in the country and raise his flowers. He's a champion grower."

Chandler nodded peacefully. "Any children?"

"No. I don't think she ever wanted any. Strange, isn't it?"

Without waiting for his answer, Sofia finished painting the picture of her aunt, and by the time they entered the town of Enghien, the subject had been changed. Slowly, the car wound its way around the lake, which shone in the sunlight like millions of diamonds. Then they headed for the residential area. Aunt Lilly's house was quite lovely, surrounded by beautiful gardens of roses and carnations, along with an enormous fir tree that dominated the yard.

From the first moment, Aunt Lilly fell under the spell of Chandler's charm. He kissed her cheek, called her Aunt Lilly, shook Nanny's hand warmly, alternately praising one's flowers and the other's housekeeping. In no time, he was part of the family. *You'd think he'd known them all his life.* What an actor, thought Sofia.

The sunlight streamed into the living room through two large bay windows. The fine old furniture stood out impressively against the white stucco walls.

Sofia managed a smile for her aunt.

"What a beautiful home, Aunt Lilly," said Chandler sincerely. "It's very much like the home of a woman who is young at heart, and it suits you perfectly. Sofia told me you do watercolors. You must show me your work when you have time. Painting has always fascinated me."

A sigh of relief escaped Sofia. She couldn't remember having seen her aunt more radiant. She was a tiny woman, with a delicate face, bright eyes, and a quick step. Her black eyes contrasted sharply with her halo of white hair. Her clothes were not in style, but such things went unnoticed, overshadowed as they were by the strength and rarity of her personality.

"If you want to talk painting, we're going to get along

marvelously! And may I tell you that I think you're a very attractive young man?" And turning to Sofia, "And you're a very lucky girl, my dear. You are beautiful together. That dress looks lovely on you. Obviously, marriage agrees with you."

Sofia blushed, while Chandler was delighted.

"You're right. I've never seen her looking better. And if you only knew how marvelous she really is," Chandler interrupted.

"I know very well, my boy. You don't have to tell me about Sofia's qualities. I'm delighted to see that you could bring her out of her shell. It's what she'd always needed . . . come, lunch is ready."

Chandler was clearly taken by this little woman, with her simple, straightforward manner. Lunch was a great success. He helped himself to two servings of the wonderful food, and even went back for thirds of Lilly's pie. Nanny, too, was enchanted with him.

After everyone had their coffee, they toured the garden, stopping at the carriage house that had been converted into a workshop for Lilly. The place was filled with paintings of roses and carnations. The old woman's talent was evident. Her colors were brilliant, her lines bold and graceful. Chandler admired her work unreservedly and his knowledgeable comments won over Lilly completely.

"Too bad you can't stay overnight," she said, as they walked back to the house. "The weather seems to be taking a turn for the worse." The sky that had been blue and beautiful in the morning had become a dreary gray. The breeze died completely, and the air was so heavy it seemed difficult to breathe.

"Aunt Lilly, I think we'd better be on our way before it storms," suggested Sofia, trying to hide her nervousness.

"You might as well wait till it blows over, dear. Those

clouds look as though they'll burst any minute now. I'll have Nanny serve us drinks."

They went back to the living room. Outside, birds fluttered in a panic, rushing to find shelter. The thunder could be heard rumbling far off in the distance. It seemed to be heading straight for Aunt Lilly's place.

"A thunderstorm," Lilly declared. "Well, I'm not surprised. My garden could use some rain, although I hope it won't be too violent."

"I hate thunderstorms," said Sofia, her voice shaky. The moment was lost for Sophia and again she surveyed her surroundings.

"You'll just have to put up with it, dear girl," said Lilly in a reassuring voice.

Chandler noticed her fright and moved to comfort her, putting his arm protectively around Sofia's shoulders. The conservation started again. It was growing late, and she kept glancing out the window, worry on her face. Dark black clouds now blanketed the sky, and suddenly, trees and branches started to sway, scattering dead and broken limbs about the grounds as the wind began blowing in gusts. Leaves were swept up and tossed in the air like paper, and then the rain came down.

"Don't be afraid, my pet," Chandler said. "I'll be your lightning rod and save you from any harm!"

Sofia's eyes widened. Unaware of what she was doing, she leaned back her head against his shoulder, and smiled. His touch was comforting, his strength reassuring. She was quite at ease, yet couldn't suppress a faint stirring of surprise at the feeling. She realized she liked the smell of his cologne, the aroma of his expensive clothes. Everything about him was masculine, and it suited him delectably.

Chandler was watching her in much the same manner an adult would look at a frightened child that needed to be treated with kindness.

Jasper never affected me this way. In any case, Jasper would never put his arm around her like this. Instead, he would have expounded on a theory of atmospheric electricity and considered her reaction silly and childish.

"It's so silly of me to be acting this way, I know," she said. "It must be my nerves . . ."

"You're not the first person to be frightened by a thunderstorm, my pet. It's nothing to be ashamed of."

Sofia cast him a grateful glance.

"My, I can see that you love to be pampered by your husband," Lilly said. "Now really, you can't possibly think of leaving in such weather. I'll see what Nanny can come up with for supper."

Lilly left the room and Chandler leaned forward. "Comfortable?" he asked Sofia solicitously.

"Yes, Chandler. Are you?" She turned the statement a bit. She wanted to stay with him all night, to feel his warmth and security from the storm outside. Much like the storm inside. Then she thought, she and Chandler were supposed to be a married couple, and that meant in the same bed—together.

"I've never been happier in my life . . ." Chandler hugged Sofia close to him.

"Right after dinner, we must leave," Sofia said in a light tone. "You do realize that, don't you, Chandler?"

"I quite understand, and I promise, if it's possible, my pet . . ."

All smiles, Lilly reentered the room, bearing good news. "For supper, I propose Chuck-eye steaks, medium rare, baked potatoes, and for dessert, rice pudding."

"Wonderful!" exclaimed Chandler. "I'm starving."

Sofia said nothing. Her mind tumbled inside itself in a frenzy, with no words making it to her tongue.

"I can hardly dine with you this way, Sofia." He moved against her, urging her answer.

Sofia exhaled a deep breath and shifted her head sideways. There was nothing to do now but let him and Lilly have their way.

Nanny's rice pudding was unlike anything he had ever eaten. The rice was topped with a layer of applesauce and, above that, whipped egg whites browned in the oven. "You really are spoiling us, Aunt Lilly," said Sofia, getting up from the table. "But the storm seems to be over and we really must be on our way."

"You must be mad, Sofia, to expect your husband to drive in this kind of weather, especially with a person sitting next to him who jumps every time there's a little thunder. It would be very dangerous, dear girl. And by the looks of things, this storm isn't going away till morning. Look outside."

The garden was a mess, its flowers bent and broken, branches of the trees twisted eerily, the pathways under water. The world below seemed to have taken on a copper color and the clouds on top were blacker than ever. The rain descended in sheets, driven by the strong wind. Lilly was right. But Sofia wasn't about to give up.

"Aunt Lilly, I'm so sorry, but I have to be in the office by nine in the morning," she begged. "You know I'd stay if I could." Her gaze shifted slowly from her aunt to Chandler. She was feeling a bit too dazed to understand what they were saying. It was clear that the moment was lost for her.

"If that's all that's worrying you, I'll call Parlay, myself. He'll understand perfectly why you're late."

Sofia turned her back on Chandler in frustration. *There is no talking to him.*

"If you please, Sofia," he smiled mockingly. "Are you not feeling better?"

Anger shook her.

Lilly was a strict Catholic woman. In a panic, Sofia looked at Chandler, but he just smiled and said nothing. But whether he would or not had nothing to do with Sofia's cause for anxiety. It wasn't the thunderstorm that was frightening her so. It was something else altogether. She knew she would be in the same bed with Chandler. Her loss of self-control would be out the window with the storm. It wasn't that she wanted to end their sexual relationship—they were in her aunt's house. If her aunt ever found out the truth, Sofia would be ashamed of herself.

Lilly broke the silence, "You see, my dear, it's impossible for you to leave in this kind of weather. Come, look. It's getting late, and you know I like to retire early. Your room is ready, and I'll give you one of my nightgowns. As for you, Chandler, well, that might be a bit more difficult. Anyway, go on up. You know where the room is, Sofia."

All her life, every time Aunt Lilly came around, it was always the smell. This scared Sofia for life. Sofia was shocked at how much her aunt had changed lately. This was the same woman she loved to avoid, growing up as a child in her own home. Every weekend Sofia was forced to go along with her parents. She couldn't bear the thought of going into the house. Aunt Lilly had a nasty habit of eating sardines. You could smell those gross little things two blocks away. They would be in open cans laying all over the kitchen, and it stank up the entire house.

Their room was beautiful. It had an enormous bed, a dressing table, a small sofa, and an adjoining bathroom. Once again, Sofia was the victim of circumstance over which she had no control. What could she do? Again, and again, lightning flashed across the sky. Thunder rolled, with rain pounding the windows. Cruel gusts of wind flung leaves and branches against the house. Lilly was right about them staying and not leaving in the middle of a storm.

There were bound to be flash floods and dangerous road conditions. Sofia turned to Chandler. He was busy like a bee, getting ready for bed. The entire situation seemed to be another something that had no hard meaning for him, a just do it and get it over with kind of attitude.

Terrified, Sofia heard her aunt come in.

"Here's one of my nightgowns, dear. It may not be as nice as yours, but it will have to do in a pinch. And here are some slippers for you, too." Lilly placed everything on the sofa. "Now, sleep well. I'll call you two for breakfast, I'll have fresh, hot, buttered buns. And which would you rather have? Tea? Coffee? Hot chocolate?"

"Anything is good for us, Aunt Lilly. We really appreciate you going through all this trouble because of us." Satisfied at last that everything was in order, Lilly turned to say, "Goodnight, all. If you need anything just yell."

"Goodnight, Aunt Lilly," Sofia replied. *As if such a thing was possible.* Once Lilly had left the room, Sofia stood motionless, looking at Chandler,

"What are we going to do now?" Sofia blurted out, her voice loud and flat.

"Come on, Sofia, this isn't the first night we've slept together. Now, go and get ready in the bathroom. Do you mind if I go have a cigarette while I'm waiting?"

Sofia turned to face Chandler, the color draining from her cheeks. "Waiting, what for?" she demanded. "And oh, I don't do well with smoking or smokers."

"To use the bathroom, silly. Why are you so nervous? Stop jumping every time I say something. And as for the smoking, I really don't smoke, I wanted to see what your take on it was."

Sofia smiled to herself, thinking of that, and her spirits rose, if only slightly. The mere thought of going home soothed her frayed nerves and she relaxed onto the pillows.

"I just might take you in my arms right now. I've been wanting all evening to get you to myself."

She didn't want to close the door, she wanted Chandler to see her, to watch her every move, touch and anything else that went along. Sofia had been waiting to hear those words, or something close all night. She was afraid he knew exactly what she was thinking. For a moment, she lay speechless. Then she turned and fled into the bathroom, closing the door behind her.

When Sofia came out, she was covered to the neck in her aunt's nightgown and gray housecoat. What an outfit! There was nothing sexy about it. For a newly married couple, she thought her aunt could have gussied it up a bit.

She restrained the impulse. A few seconds later she could hear the water running in the bathroom and Chandler quietly humming. He was gazing out the window. He didn't turn around as Sofia slipped into bed. She felt so embarrassed about the gown and had the childish desire to hide her head under the blanket.

Of course, this was all amusing to Chandler, Sofia thought, furious at his apparent lack of concern. She decided to pretend to be asleep when he came out of the bath, but she couldn't resist opening one eye for a peek. He was incredibly luscious!

He emerged wearing the most incredible pajamas she'd ever seen. Covered with big red hearts, they resembled the outfit of a Harlequin in love. Amazingly, there was still something distinctly elegant about Chandler!

It was growing colder, the wind seeping into the room through cracks between the glass and the window frame. Sofia watched him ramble awkwardly onto the sofa, trying to stretch his legs. She felt sorry for him.

"Chandler," she called out lightly, "you're going to freeze

to death on that sofa, and I'm awfully warm in here. Take the bedspread off the bed. You'll be more comfortable." What was she saying? Chandler needed to be beside her, not at the foot of the bed.

"Ah! And here I thought you were asleep. How considerate of you about my welfare. Thanks anyway, but I'm just fine." Then he asked, "Aren't you afraid of the thunder anymore? It's still rolling out there. Don't you want me to sit with you and hold you?"

What words to her ears! "Oh, no, Chandler," she stammered, "that won't be necessary." What in the hell had she just done? A perfect opportunity out the window with the damn storm.

"Don't get me wrong, I would only hold your hand until you fall asleep. You know, the way it's done with small children."

"No, you can stay where you are . . . are you sure you're comfortable enough? I mean, I want to, but my aunt and—"

"Not as comfortable as I would be next to you . . . alright, alright. Relax. I'll keep my distance."

Sofia rolled her head towards Chandler, then raised up to look at him before saying, "What did you say?"

"I said, good freaking night, darling, and I won't take back a single word. Those are all the things young husbands say, I believe, even when their wives make them sleep on the sofa. Sleep well."

Sofia wanted badly for Chandler to be at her side. She craved his warmth, his touch, to feel his lips upon hers. She was empty and in furious need of filling. No one could hear, or even care if they did hear. They want to hear the love between newlyweds. She sighed a deep breath, keeping her thoughts just that—thoughts.

The next morning, an orange hot radiance streamed

down, enough to wake anyone right away. The sun was bright and smothering the entire room with light. When Sofia woke, she opened her eyes without moving. The room was still and quiet and she thought she was alone. She noticed that Chandler wasn't on the sofa and couldn't hear the water running in the bathroom. She scrambled out of bed and ran to the window. There he was, in the garden below, walking with Lilly, checking to see what the damage the storm had done. He was fully dressed, even to the jacket of his gray suit, and Lilly was dressed as usual in black and wearing wooden shoes that she appeared to be able to walk in with ease.

Tiny drops of moisture dribbled down the window sill, and covered the leaves of the trees, sparkling in the sunlight like diamonds. Toward the back of the yard Downey, the gardener, was raking the leaves and gathering the branches that were broken from the trees. Overall, the garden didn't appear to have suffered a lot of damage.

Chandler was trying to be amusing and, under the circumstances, she couldn't be angry with him. Sofia felt happy and more relaxed now that the night was over. It hadn't been all that bad. He had been very considerate and tactful in their situation, although he might have dispensed with some of the teasing. That was Chandler, all right.

Sofia opened the window, took a deep breath and, as Aunt Lilly and Chandler looked up, shouted, "I'll be down in a few minutes."

"No hurry, dear," Lilly called back. "Parlay isn't expecting you until this afternoon. When you're ready, we'll have breakfast."

But, unaccountably, Sofia was very anxious to join them, and practically threw her clothes on.

It wasn't until they were on their way back to Paris that

Chandler brought up the subject of their night, and again, she felt embarrassed.

"Let's not talk about it, please. We weren't responsible for what happened, and I feel bad about it." Chandler knew Sofia didn't want to stay with her aunt, it was his fault. The only thing at this point was to let it lie and go on with the day.

But could Sofia? She kept remembering what Chandler had called her. "My precious one, my beautiful one, my darling . . ." What had she done to deserve a man like him? Her love was growing by the minute. She didn't want to ever see herself without him by her side, and she would do whatever she had to see that he stayed.

CHAPTER SEVEN

It was Sofia's day back at work and she never expected anything but a normal work day, after the incident with Chandler. She noticed the lights were off. The lights were to never be turned off, per Parlay's orders. He had a thing about walking into a dark room, since he had been mugged ten years ago in the very same building. It was a red flag, but Sofia had Chandler on her mind, not work, and continued without thinking.

Sofia fumbled with the keys and gently opened the door, but she peeped inside before actually going in. She gently opened the door and reached for the light switch. As soon as she flipped the switch, people popped up from every corner, empty space and behind her desk.

"Congratulations Sofia!" If it weren't yelled a dozen times, she heard it once with horns blowing, streamers scattered and enough snack food and cake to feed the entire block. The tables were scattered with platters of chicken salad finger sandwiches cut in cute little triangle shapes, homemade chocolate cookies with the cross-fork design in the center, cherry punch made with sherbet and ginger ale in a giant traditional punch bowl with a dipper and glasses, and spiked with the best Vodka in the country Parlay had sprung for. The napkins had matching spoons & forks wrapped in the cutest way to display the décor, while one table stood alone with wrapped gifts, adorned with ribbon and bows, stuffed with secret somethings inside.

Trying to get her composure together, there was one thing

that took Sofia's breath away. It was a wedding cake, a three-tier, with a little bride and groom adorning the top tier with surrounding flowers of Sofia's favorite. It was a traditional white cake with beautiful array of colored flowers draping each tier. She teared up and couldn't find the words. No one had ever done such a beautiful thing for her. She had never expected anything like this, and it was all for her. She was trying to get the words out, but her tears prevented anything but muffled sobs.

"Not a word, Ms. Sofia." Parlay stepped up, to be the first one to speak. "Sofia, don't say a word." Parlay hesitated. "We all are so proud of you. You've been a valuable employee to the company, and we consider you as a part of our family. Everyone thought you could use a few things as a newlywed. It's not a wedding shower, mind you. So, I'm not going to say another word and let the party commence." Parlay walked the room, making sure all were having a good time, eating and drinking their fill.

It was a little late for a party, because she had already been back a few days, but she said nothing, smiled and went along as any blushing new bride should.

"Is the punch spiked?" Sofia yelled above everyone, holding up her cup with a smile as wide as the Grand Canyon. Never had anyone ever done anything like this for her. Always a bridesmaid and never a bride—until now.

Sofia's parents divorced when she was just eleven, and as soon as she was eighteen she was handed her walking papers. She's grown a thick skin quickly, and almost never allowed anything nor anyone in.

At the end of the day Sofia was exhausted. She'd been off for a few days and was trying to get back into the swing of things, but the party took center stage this day, and that was no problem. As hard as she tried, she couldn't reach Chandler, and for the first time, they made love in her mind.

She'd always wanted a man like Chandler, and now she had him.

When the whistle announced the end of the day, people could be heard rushing about, exchanging goodbyes in the hallways while Sofia put away the files on her desk.

Parlay was watching Sofia with a concerned look all day, and saying nothing. It was clear he had something on his mind. He wanted to speak with her before she left.

"Is something wrong, Mr. Parlay?" Sofia asked, both brows drawn inward in question.

"Everything is fine, as far as the business is concerned, So-fia . . . but I'm worried about Frances."

"Frances?"

"Yes. Frances Shawna." He gave Sofia a strange look.

"Ah, Frances," replied Sofia, who had always addressed the woman as Meme. She was in her mid-forties, and Sofia considered her advanced enough in years to be afforded the respect reserved for an older person.

"You know her, don't you, Sofia?"

"Of course, though most of my recollections come from other people who know her better. She's in accounts receivable. I don't really deal with her. But she's been off work for a little while. Is she okay or needing anything?"

"Yeah, she's on sick leave right now, and that is what is worrying me. She's a brave woman, and I'm afraid her illness is more serious than she's saying." Parlay described a person that was seriously ill and knew but hadn't told anyone, due to her respect.

Sofia looked away, recoiling from the sharpness, however justified, and shut down her computer.

Parlay hesitated a moment. "Are you busy tonight?"

"Not particularly. I'm just going home." A feeling of unease fluttered briefly in Sofia's stomach but faded when she looked at Parlay.

"I'd like to know how Frances is getting along," continued Parlay. "Would it be too inconvenient for you to drop by her place on your way home?"

Sofia smiled nervously but didn't answer immediately.

"She lost her husband two years ago. Her parents live in the south and are a bit old for travel. She'd had no one to check on her."

"Doesn't she have a little girl?" She stood undecided for a moment.

"A seven-year-old she had after twenty years of marriage. If she's bedridden, I'm wondering how she can manage with such a young child. I'd appreciate it very much if you could drop in and check on her. Of course, I'll pay for your cab fare there and back. She lives quite a distance from the office here and even farther from your place."

The prospect of a visit didn't appeal to Sofia. If she arrived home too late, she'd miss seeing Chandler. She had noticed lately that she was anxious to get home before he went out. Nevertheless, her natural kindness wouldn't allow her to ignore a person in distress.

"Sure, I'll drop by to see her and call you later to let you know how she is. I'm sure she'll be happy to know you're concerned about her." Sofia hesitated, "What's her address?"

A look of relief crossed Parlay's face and he quickly wrote down the street and number, then handed it to Sofia, together with some money for cab fare, and he thanked her.

"I know how reliable you are, Sofia, and that you'll be honest and tell me exactly what is wrong with her," he stressed. "This isn't something I would ask just anyone to do."

"I know, Mr. Parlay. I know."

He smiled and left her without saying any more.

At the end of the day Sofia left, a little daunted by the prospect of missing a chance to see Chandler, but happy to be able to do a favor for her boss. She had a great deal of respect for Parlay and felt guilty about her deception. If this visit could make up for some of what she had done, it certainly would be worth it.

Frances lived in a one-bedroom apartment in a fourth-floor walkup. By the time Sofia reached the door, she was out of breath. Maybe if she were in better shape her body wouldn't try to shut down. Meme was wearing a housecoat, her hair unkempt, when she opened the door.

"Oh, Sofia," she said, "how nice of you to come by! Please, come in. I'll bet Parlay sent you, didn't he?"

Sofia smiled, her attention drawn to the way Meme was dressed.

"I'll be right back, sweetie."

"Goodness, Ms. Meme, how are you feeling?" she asked with concern. While she explained the reason for her visit, Sofia followed her through the living room and into the bedroom, where there were two beds—a large one and a small one.

Seated in front of a table was a small child playing with her stuffed animals. She was a lovely child, with blonde curls and large brown eyes.

"This is my daughter," Meme said, proudly. "Lynn, this is Sofia, hello. We work together at the plant." She looked happy to introduce her.

"Oh! You don't have to disturb her," Sofia said quickly.

Lynn looked up at her and smiled. She saw Sofia and motioned for her to join her.

"Well, hello, Lynn. It's nice to meet you. What lovely toys you have there! I see you have a lot of cows and horses. I love horses, they are my favorite."

"I have a pony, too," said Lynn, "and some chickens." She smiled gently. "Will you take me to ride sometime, Ms.

Sofia?"

"Lynn, we don't ask others to do things. You go in the next room and take your toys," Meme ordered her gently.

"That's okay Meme, I'll take her for a ride sometime, if you'll allow it," Sofia said somberly.

"Oh, mommy can I, can I go with Ms. Sofia?" Little Lynn begged as any child would.

"That will be up to Ms. Sofia. I know you'll be safe with her." Meme agreed.

"The next time I go, I'll come get you. Okay?" Sofia smiled and patted Lynn on the back.

Lynn would have been happy to go on forever, but Frances was inviting Sofia to take a chair beside the bed.

By the end of an hour, Sofia had forgotten entirely about Chandler. She had been completely captivated by the little girl and was concerned about the state of her mother's health.

"It was very nice of Parlay to send you," she said, "and just as nice of you to come. Thank you, Sofia. I've always liked you—you're such a pleasant person and seem so levelheaded."

Levelheaded? Not any more, she wasn't! Would a level-headed girl take a stranger into her apartment, have won-derfully wild sex, and then fall for him? Sofia felt like spew-ing the truth all over the room. Sofia shook her head and managed a faint smile. "I'm not always so practical."

"Oh! You mean about Jasper? Of course, at first, we were all surprised. And the poor boy was so unhappy. But he wasn't for you. Did you know that none of us ever thought he was? And your husband is so charming."

"Have you met Chandler?"

"No, but one of the girls called last night. Everyone loves him. Parlay was talking about him. We are all happy for you, Sofia. It's so hard to be alone these days."

"So, you know about the commotion he was in the middle of last week?"

"I do."

"Pretty bad, huh?" Sofia remarked with her head down in shame.

"On the contrary, I just wished I could have been there! Honey, we all love Chandler, even Parlay and his family."

"Really?"

"Really. You have you a fine young man. He's a keeper, no doubt."

Frances proceeded to tell Sofia all about her current dilemma. She was going to have a surgery. It was not what she wanted, but her issues were out of control and it seemed the only way to take care of the problem. She worried about what to do with Lynn. She needed someone to take care of her daughter during her stay in the hospital and her recovery period.

"My neighbors are very kind and will do my shopping for me. While I'm at work I have someone who comes in to take care of Lynn. She'd be able to get her meals, but I can't ask her to keep Lynn overnight. A social worker offered to take her, but where would she place her? Hell, Sofia, would I get her back? I can't trust someone like that.

"I thought about the At the Children's Aid home, and what if I am a little slow recovering from the surgery? I'm afraid I want to get her back, it's my main concern right now.

"She might be thrown together with children in some welfare agency. My doctor keeps telling me that it isn't good for me to worry, but how can I help it? I need to find someone, a couple or a family, to look after Lynn while I'm in the hospital. When you're a mother, Sofia, you'll understand exactly where this is coming from."

Frances' child, the only precious thing she had in her life.

The child was so adorable, with her pink cheeks and brown eyes. From time to time, Lynn could be heard imitating animal sounds as she led the toys to the barn or the pond.

Sofia's heart contracted in sympathy, only there wasn't anything she could do for Lynn.

"Just thinking that Lynn might be taken away by some welfare agency is destroying me," continued Frances, her voice faint and hesitant. "Everyone I know goes to work, even you, Sofia. There's one family on the floor below, but they're always on holidays. It's so disheartening to be alone at time like this."

Sofia had been deeply moved when Frances said *Everyone I know goes to work. Even you.* She would have been happy to look after Lynn, but unfortunately, she wasn't home during the day, either.

Sofia sighed with regret. All she could do was try to offer comfort. And after making sure that Frances had everything she needed, Sofia left, feeling almost as desperate as the heartsick mother she was leaving behind. The idea of Parlay sending her now surfaced. He knew what spot Frances was in and needed a sitter for her little Lynn. But Sofia couldn't take the child, either, and anyone to put it on her intentionally was wrong. Parlay knew exactly what he was doing, and Sofia was not happy with him. No consideration for that in the least.

Sofia had stayed longer than she had intended, and already had to wait a long time before she got a taxi, so it was quite late when she arrived home. She had stopped thinking about Chandler long enough to get her bearings straight. He might be gone by the time she got home.

Tired and upset with Parlay, Sofia was bothered because she couldn't do more for Meme. She inserted her key into her lock, but before she could turn it the door was whipped open. She found herself confronted by Chandler, a furious look on his face.

"Well," he said, "this is a fine time to be getting home from work! I've been waiting for over an hour, listening for the elevator! Did you get lost or what?"

Speechless with surprise, she just stood and stared at him. *Where was this coming from?* This was proving there is another side to Chandler and why he wasn't married. *Is this the real Chandler?*

"And don't try to tell me you've been shopping or something," Chandler went on, "it's long past the time when the stores close."

"Who the hell said anything about shopping?" she mumbled, more and more confused.

"I suppose you've been running around with that ex-fiancé of yours, what's-his-name."

"Chandler! What on earth's got into you?" she snapped, "and keep your voice down, I don't want anyone hearing us argue. This situation is awkward enough."

"Nothing! At least, well, it's just that I don't like the idea of your running about with other men."

"Oh God, Chandler, you couldn't be more wrong!" She bit his head completely off. "Don't you ever accuse me of being with another man. If I were, I can guarantee you'd be the first to know."

"Alright, then," Chandler said, trying to calm down. "I have to admit you don't look happy about something. If your boyfriend stood you up, don't expect to come crying to me." Quietly he added, "Well, was it Jasper?"

"Fuck, Chandler, for God's sake will you shut the hell up with Jasper! I just got back from Meme's—" She tried to explain, but Chandler wouldn't shut up long enough and kept interrupting her when tried to explain.

As she started to speak, his anger visibly gave way to interest, then to genuine concern.

"I'm sorry, Sofia, very sorry. I can't imagine another man

even looking at you. You should have told me right away."

"You didn't give me a chance, and by the way, while we're on this, you don't own me. This whole shenanigan has cost me, *me*, Chandler," she blurted angrily. "Besides, you jumped me as soon as I came through the door. Don't you dare do that to me again. If I were seeing anyone, I'd have the decency to tell you. I don't go behind anyone's back with anything, including an affair. I don't do it and I would like to know if it were happening to me. Besides, men make it a point to never kiss and tell.

"Meme is a coworker and is home sick and must go in the hospital. She must have surgery and needs someone to look after her little girl for a few days. I know she was asking me, but I can't take care of a little girl, I have to work."

Chandler didn't address that response, but he did this one. "I know, and I was wrong. I was so worried about you! If I had known, I would have greeted you differently. Look, I hope you told her we'd be glad to look after little girl. Did you?"

"How could I? I don't know anything about taking care of children, Chandler. You can't be serious. It's a child. Do you? Because if you do, then maybe you should take care of her."

"I can look after her till you get home," he replied calmly.

Sofia looked at him with dismay. "You? You've got to be kidding?"

"Why should I be kidding? I very seldom leave the apartment during the day. When I must leave, it's in the evening, and you are home by then. Surely we can arrange something. We'll talk to your boss about it in the morning."

"Don't you dare speak to my boss about this, it's my life, and it's not controlled by anyone but me. Besides, you wouldn't mind this, any of this?"

"Of course not! I adore children. I keep telling you that.

Most of the time, they love me, too. Didn't you notice that the night we were at the Parlays for dinner?"

"I did, but that was only for a short time. To keep a little girl and take care of her all day is different. You don't know anything about children."

"What do you mean? It's not rocket science to watch a kid. You're the one trying to make me out to be illiterate or something. I love children," he replied, as though he had been gravely offended.

This time, silence was a virtue, and for a moment, Sofia froze, and slowly, she took hold of herself. Chandler had spoken with such conviction that there could be no doubt. It had come straight from the heart, and that was what hurt the most.

"One child?" she murmured faintly. "But you've never mentioned anything about them."

"No, no children."

"Then you're married?"

"I'm neither married nor divorced. And I'm not a widower either. As a matter of fact, I'm not even engaged." Chandler fixed Sofia with a steady gaze. "As I told you before, I'm a bachelor, as free as a bird!"

Sofia looked at him in complete bewilderment. "I cannot believe you are wanting to do this. I'm not the kid type, and I've told you this."

"I know," he said, smiling. "It's a little complicated. Don't try to understand it just now. It isn't important. What is important right now is rescuing that poor woman. Tomorrow is Saturday, and you don't have to work. So come along. Let's concern ourselves with the problem. What would you do if you were in the same position?"

Sofia tried to rid her mind of disturbing thoughts. "You know, Chandler, you have a way of making things very difficult for me at times," she said with dread. "As to the problem, I don't know where the child would even sleep. I have no bed for her." She stared so hard at his chest shew as surprised it didn't burst into flame.

"We'll bring hers with us, or she can sleep in my bed, and I'll sleep with you. What's wrong with that?"

"Fine," Sofia exhaled. "I can't believe I let you talk me into this. I'll call Parlay in a minute and let him set it up to pick Lynn up."

"We'll go together, in the car. Everything will work out just fine, you'll see."

Sofia was far from being convinced, and her sleep was troubled enough.

But the next morning, when she saw Chandler full of enthusiasm, her fears vanished. She even stopped worrying and decided it had been just another one of his jokes. She felt pleased he was being so generous and considerate.

It would be Jasper who wouldn't help an elderly woman across the street—he'd push her in front of a bus and say, *oops, I didn't see her standing there.*

As Chandler spoke to Sofia, he took her gently by the arm. "Come on, dear. Let's go out and buy some toys for Lynn to play with. She won't feel so unwanted here while away from her mother. I noticed that there's a shop close by that's sure to have toys and children's things."

"That's a good idea, they'll keep her busy anyway." Sofia stopped. "Oh, she likes to ride horses like me, so if you could find a farm, I told her that I'd take her one day." Sofia spoke up as she remembered what she had told her.

Despite his mischievous tone, Sofia could sense Chandler's determination and decided not to argue. He looked so happy. Why spoil his fun?

When they reached the department store, Sofia followed Chandler to see what he would do. Scarcely had he set foot in the department when three young salesgirls materialized. He wasn't looking for advice nor admirers. He knew exactly what he wanted, and in no time, he added a kitchen set with an oven that worked, a three-foot-tall teddy bear, and some educational games.

Moving quickly from one counter to another, as though money was of no concern, he made all his purchases with ease and savoir faire.

"She'll be tickled to death, Chandler," Sofia laughed. "All this must have cost a small fortune."

"Now don't start fussing about money," he answered. "The important thing is that the child will be happy while she is with us, and if we only give her toys like ones she already has, she wouldn't be very impressed. In fact, she probably wouldn't even be interested at all. That is why there are so many here. We want to make sure she will come back and stay with us again."

"So, we're buying the kid off with toys, so she'll come back?" Sofia commented, knowing good well Chandler knew what she was getting at.

"I'd come back if I were the kid getting all these toys," the little cashier butted in, with a smile from here to the north pole.

"I don't recall anyone asking you, Miss." Sofia allowed herself a bit of self-recognition.

"Sofia," Chandler whispered in disgust. Once more, Chandler demonstrated his ability to mesh with people from all walks of life.

Upon their arrival at Meme's, Chandler spoke to Meme with warmth and concern, and Lynn allowed him to pick her up into his arms. He explained wholeheartedly to her that she had all kinds of new toys to play with at his and Sofia's place, and that they are going to take her horseback riding.

Chandler told Lynn that she could call him her Uncle Boo, and that he and Sofia had come to take her on a holiday, so her mother could get her much-needed rest when she came home from the hospital.

Lynn's bed came apart for easy travel. Meme had bought it with that concern.

Chandler overheard, and yelled aloud that Lynn had a bed all ready to sleep in and that all she needed was her suitcase.

Always with a smile, Chandler went up and down several flights of stairs three times, after which he crammed Lynn's suitcase in the trunk of the car. Lynn could sit in the back seat in her seatbelt.

Meanwhile, Sofia gathered up Lynn's pillow and one of her toys to take along to play with in the car.

Meme was able to help a little. Now that the worry of what was going to happen to her child no longer burdened her, she seemed somewhat perkier. Her voice had become stronger, her eyes brighter, and her cheeks had taken on a little color.

Sofia was happy with the outcome of Meme's concerns. She came alive when she knew who Lynn was going to be with.

"Your husband has been sent from heaven," she told Sofia, while Chandler was making one of his trips to the car. "And he's as handsome as he is good. You're very lucky."

So many people had been telling her the same thing. Sofia was starting to believe it. With Chandler, everything was simpler, brighter, and easier. "This won't be forever, Frances," he said. "I'll bring your daughter to see you at the hospital every day, and in the meantime, we'll take very good care of her. Now, you rest and try not to think about anything but getting well."

If Lynn felt any shyness when she first walked into the

apartment, it was quickly dissipated by the excitement and joy of opening the huge box of new toys. She ran back and forth between the teddy bear and the doll, kissing the first one and then the other, not knowing which she preferred. Then she spread everything out on the floor, chattering to herself and her new friends.

CHAPTER EIGHT

That night, Lynn was quite content. Sofia had run her a bubble bath and put toys in to play with as she bathed her and washed her hair. Lynn had a ball playing in the bubbles.

"I've never had a bath like this, Ms. Sofia," Lynn said shyly, but her face lit up like a Christmas tree when she had seen them.

"I'll be right here, Lynn, to get you out and dry your hair. You just have some fun, I'll be right here if you need anything," Sofia explained, but all she could see was the fun Lynn was having splashing around in the bubbles with her toys.

"Chandler," Sofia whispered, while calling out for him.

"What," he replied loudly.

"Shhhhh!" Sofia said, and put her finger over her lips.

"What," he whispered.

"Lynn has never had a bubble bath before." Sofia was surprised. "I can't believe that. A simple bubble bath." Sofia couldn't believe what Lynn said to her. She scratched the top of her head and returned to dry Lynn down and put her hair up before going to bed.

"My mommy has never dried my hair like this." Lynn perked up while playing with a horse.

"How does she dry your hair?" Sofia stopped and asked as she leaned over her shoulder.

"When it gets wet, she only dries a little bit with a towel." She continued to play.

Sofia was a little caught off-guard with Lynn's answer. She finished drying her hair and then brushed her teeth before putting her to bed.

"Miss Sofia," Lynn spoke up with her bright little eyes.

"Yes?"

"Thank you for letting me stay with you and Uncle Boo. I didn't want to go with Miss Carol. She has all kinds of bugs in her house, and I never get to take a bath."

Oh, dear Lord, Sofia thought, and she turned her head to hide the tears when she noticed Chandler in the closet. She continued making comments, ignoring his presence

"Well, we take a bath here, and a bubble one, too." Sofia continued as she'd heard nothing. After finishing, Sofia tucked Lynn in. She dropped off to sleep the minute her head hit the pillow.

Lynn slept soundly, well into the morning.

Chandler was preparing breakfast, and it filled the apartment with scents of bacon and biscuits in the oven.

"Ahhh, sleeping beauty has risen," Chandler teased when Sofia walked into the living room.

As it was Sunday morning, Chandler and Sofia took Lynn to noon Mass, where she was very well-behaved. In the afternoon, they visited the zoo, and Lynn was delighted by all the different animals.

The following morning, Sofia was a little apprehensive about having to go to work and leave Lynn in Chandler's care. After going over lists and emergency numbers three times, Sofia left for work—not that she was of much use to anyone there, with her mind on Chandler and Lynn. After work, she hurried back to the apartment.

"Well, how did it go today with you and Lynn?"

"Everything's fine, my pet. She's a charming little girl, and I've never had so much fun. What did you think I was going to do?"

"I don't know, I was just asking. It must have been a tiring day for you."

"Nonsense! It's too soon to go to the hospital to see her mother, since Meme was operated on this morning. I called, and everything seems to have gone well. Lynn and I have made all sorts of plans—the Luxemburg Palace, the Tuilleries Gardens—visits we'll make accompanied by Emma and Tiger. Those are the names she has given to her doll and teddy bear. Would you believe it? We're having quite a time for ourselves."

Sofia couldn't remember ever having seen Chandler so happy—or herself, for that matter, outside the bedroom. She could scarcely believe it, but the picture of him walking around Paris with a little girl, a teddy bear, and a doll carriage was even harder to imagine.

"Chandler! Are you really going to be spending your days showing her the city and carrying her around?"

"Of course I am! You've been trying to find me a job, haven't you? Well, being a babysitter suits me just fine. We can talk about it later. Right now, I must leave. It's your turn to play the role of parent." Chandler had spoken the words very gently, and before leaving, he turned back to say something else. Sofia detected the emotion in his voice.

"And I'm sure it's a role that would suit you well. Just you wait and see." He laughed.

"Oh, God." *How can I resist him? Sometimes he's so infuriating, and then he turns around and is marvelous.*

When the door closed behind him, Sofia went into the living room where Lynn was playing.

"Hi, Lynn. Did you have a nice day?"

"Oh, yes."

"Did you have a good lunch?"

This was one of the things that has been worrying Sofia most.

"We went to a restaurant, Aunt Sofia," said Lynn playing, jumping onto her knees on a trampoline. "A restaurant, I've never been to one."

She could hardly expect Chandler cooking more than eggs. Was he choosing the right kind of food for a little girl? Of course, what was she thinking, Chandler knows all sorts of things!

The child was continuing enthusiastically, "I had chicken, fresh beans, and some apple pie."

"Wow, that sounds good," said Sofia, somewhat relieved. "Did you play any games today?"

"I dropped my doll and Uncle Boo was her doctor; we played robbers too, 'cept Uncle Boo was much too clever." The little girl shook her blonde curls. "I could never tell when he was taking the money out of my pocket."

Her last words troubled Sofia. Chandler had the cunning of a thief, but she didn't consider it much of a compliment. True, with children, it was relatively easy. Sofia regained her smile as she listened to Lynn babble on about her day.

"Then he told me stories, and when I started playing with Emma and Tiger, Uncle Boo wrote some letters."

"It sounds like you had a fun day." Sofia smiled, and then twirled her gaze to Chandler.

"Oh, yes! And tomorrow, we're going to see Mama at the hospital. Uncle Boo promised."

"Well, if he promised, Lynn, then you'll go." The only thing Sofia was thinking about was Chandler, and not just Chandler, but his wedding tackle. Was she so selfish to want him to herself for a few minutes? Lynn wasn't a problem. It was because Sofia was young, single and enjoyed her men. A child wasn't on the menu and probably never would be.

There wasn't anything particularly strange about the fact Chandler was writing letters, but when the little girl mentioned it each time she was telling Sofia about her day, Sofia couldn't stop her curiosity. To whom was Chandler writing so faithfully? A woman he was in love with, maybe? Sofia shuddered at the thought. But she soon forgot about it. He was being so considerate at times, and Sofia had the delightful impression she had both a husband and a child.

At the end of two weeks, Frances was back on her feet and in her apartment, and Lynn was returned to her. The child left Sofia and Uncle Boo as easily as she had joined them. Of course, learning the beautiful new toys were hers to keep helped the transition.

"Well now," said Chandler later that evening when they were back home, "here we are, just the two of us again."

"Yeah, and thank you very much for all the help. You didn't have to do any of it. None of this would have been possible without you, though. You've been very kind and considerate, to have been able to help someone that made me feel good inside. We worked very well together."

"Really?" said Chandler, as though this was very important to him.

"Yes, really. I have to admit I'm going to miss Lynn. You've done so much when you didn't have to. You went further than I could ever could have."

There was no more laughter in the apartment, no more toys and games. No more outings, no livelier child with stories to tell. Gone were the blonde curls and rosy cheeks.

"My dear, you still have me!" exclaimed Chandler, his eyebrows raised in mockery. "Am I not just as important?"

"Don't tease me, Chandler! If you knew how nice it felt, when I came home from work, to have those little arms around my neck, feel her kisses on my cheek, hear this place filled with laughter."

"If that's what you're missing, my pet," he said seriously, still smiling, "I'll be here to give it all to you. Yes, to kiss you, put my arms around you . . . a delightful idea! Would you like me to start now?"

He hadn't moved, but Sofia stepped back. She was angry.

"You really are revolting! How can you make fun of honest emotion? Doesn't anything ever touch you? Don't you have any feelings about anything?" Sofia looked at him indignantly. Just a moment before, he had sounded enthusiastic about the idea of the two of them alone again, and now, he was back to his infernal joking. Which was the real Chandler?

"I'm sorry," he said, "but you must learn not to be so serious all the time."

He walked over to her and put his hands on her shoulders.

She showed no sign of protest.

"Listen, I know I shouldn't be making jokes right now, because you're emotional. I can understand that. That's why I don't think you should sit around here feeling sorry for yourself. No matter how horrible you think I am, I'm sure I can find something for us to do that will take your mind off Lynn. What would you say to an invitation to go out for a change of mood?"

Sofia was moved by his genuine good intention. "I'm not as sad as it may appear. It was different, but kids really are not in the cards for me. I enjoy being free, and kids only put a damper on things. Do you want to go out for dinner with me? Because if you do, let's go."

His face lit up, "Alright, then. What are we waiting for?"

The following week was one of the most enjoyable times Sofia had ever known.

Chandler took her out for dinner almost every night. He knew the restaurants of Paris well and chose them for their intimacy and décor, as well as their good food. Impressed by his elegant dress, his ease, and natural self-assurance, every maître d' jumped to see that they got the best table and were given extra special attention.

Sofia had never been spoiled this way, and it embarrassed her a little.

"You must be spending a fortune on me, Chandler."

"Don't worry about it, my dear. When this runs out, I can always get more."

"Without working?"

"Working? That's all you ever seem to talk about. Isn't being in an office all day enough, without having to think about it after you get home? Aren't we having a good time together?"

"Of course, Chandler . . . but I never knew life could be like this. Work is all I've ever done."

"Isn't a husband supposed to make sure his wife is entertained . . . take her out? You must learn to accept things as they come. I'm happy to be able to bring joy into your life. Up till now, things have been dulling, haven't they?"

It was true—until Sofia met Chandler, her life certainly had been without fun. And now she could see the end of the month approaching much too soon. She wished it could go on forever. She had fallen for her handsome stranger in the night. But he had said they would *get a divorce* after the month was over. He hadn't said anything about it lately, however. Neither had she.

Of late Sofia had begun to feel that something was growing, that was bringing them closer together. Was it physical? Emotional? She had no idea. Still, there was a quality about Chandler she had never found in any other man.

Sofia couldn't deny that Chandler was gorgeous—no, downright gorgeous—with his dark hair, bright blue eyes, and bronze tan, and that incredible smile. Intelligent, likable, cultured, his sense of humor might be infuriating at times, but it never was his intention to be offensive.

He was so alive, she thought, that he seemed to bring new life to everything around him. Chandler's ability to switch his mood from light to serious whenever the occasion demanded signified that he was a person of rare character. His slight British accent made every word music to Sofia's ears. He was so very much alive, she thought, that he seemed to bring new life to everything around him.

In addition, he had another quality that was exceptional — he understood women. He loved their company, supported their weaknesses, and admired their strengths.

Had Chandler ever been in love? *Of course he has, he must have. Stop being so silly!*

He had a way of avoiding answers to most direct questions. Despite the closeness of their relationship, Sofia still knew very little about him. She knew nothing of his past or future and very little about his present. She had noticed, however, that each time he entered a restaurant, he glanced around quickly to see who was there. One night, as Sofia preceded him, he suddenly clutched her arm and whispered, "Let's have dinner someplace else tonight."

Outside, he offered an explanation. "I saw people I knew in there, and I don't want you to meet them. Besides, the food is just as good next door. Let's go."

Somehow, that didn't seem like Chandler. Why didn't he want his friends to meet Sofia? Wasn't she good enough for them? She knew she looked very chic in her pastel yellow dress, touched off by a diamond brooch her mother had given her. Was he afraid she might find out from others what he was taking such care to keep from her? Was it something that might embarrass him? Chandler gave her one of his most dazzling smiles. "Now don't pay any mind to this, darling. Those people would have wanted us to join them, and I want you all to myself tonight. Is there anything wrong with that? Anyway, I've decided that tonight I'm going to begin a program that will add to your education."

Sofia stared at him in utter bewilderment.

"What did you say? I'm sorry, I didn't understand you."

"That's because I was speaking French, dear. You see, this morning I decided to speak to you only in English from now on. In other words, I'll be giving you English lessons. You'll find it very useful to be able to converse in two languages, you'll see. I remember you telling me that you could read English but had trouble speaking it. This will be a good way for you to learn to speak it. What do you say?"

"That's great, but you'll have to speak very slowly at first."

"Very well, darling," was his soothing response.

"And, please, none of the darling business." Sofia felt like it made her feel cheap. She had never much cared for it in the first place.

"Alright, no, darling, my pet." Chandler replied

Soon they were both laughing at the mistakes Sofia made from time to time as they continued their conversation in English. But it didn't take her long to pick up the appropriate rhythms. She had an ear for languages, and Chandler's accent was perfect.

Chandler spoke true Oxford English, and the phrase, *Oxford graduate*, came to her mind suddenly.

Surely he couldn't have studied at Oxford? Only the children of rich and aristocratic families attended the famous English university. Not that Chandler wouldn't have been a match for them, but he wouldn't have had the money. The one thing Sofia knew about his family was something he mentioned in passing. "My father was a drinker and died very young, so I owe a great deal to my mother. Despite her grief, her courage never faltered."

Sofia was becoming more and more concerned about him, and one evening, a call from Amanda caused her to worry even more. For Sofia, this brief description had conjured up sordid London neighborhoods, so well described by Dickens. Was Chandler from a working-class family, perhaps even a very poor family? It seemed incredible, but of course, entirely possible. Chandler's mother had probably worked very hard to help her son so that he could escape that environment. What had she done for a living? What was she doing now? Chandler had never said and apparently preferred not to talk about it. Being polite, Sofia had not wanted to ask. Poor, dear Chandler. He loved luxury and the easy life so much. "So, you're back from Nice? Are you engaged?"

"Engaged? Of course not!" replied Amanda furiously. "Men are all alike—pigs! That sneaky little Eric! I thought he was such a gentleman, and I was sure he was in love with me. Well, I was wrong! After fifteen days, he just up and left me! But, tell me about you. There's no one worse than the Adonis type for making promises. As far as I'm concerned, that's it. I'm never going to get married, unless I know the man very well, and even then, not until after we've been engaged for a long while. I hear that's not the way it was with you, Sofia."

No, she didn't have the courage to break off their relationship, as strange as it was. Sofia was completely demoralized. Was Chandler like other men? He was so nice. Together, they had visited the new room at the Louvre museum, had even gone to concerts. What would she do without him?

In any case, Sofia wasn't famous for her ability to exaggerate, and the next day, when Chandler arrived, saying, "Don't you think it's a little too soon to accuse me? I'm very happy with my room. Would you mind terribly if I rented it for another month?"

Sofia had been very quick to answer, "No, I wouldn't mind." She wanted to look at him and say, *there's no money required.*

"Thank you, but I have only enough money to pay you for two weeks, unfortunately. I'm broke."

"Oh dear. That's because you've been spending so much money on me. Look, I'm never home for lunch, so why don't you use the kitchen and do your own cooking instead of eating out every day?"

"Sofia, that's very kind of you, and tonight, I'm inviting you for dinner. That's the least I could do. On my way home I'll stop at the store and pick up everything we need."

"In that case, I accept."

"This is just a temporary setback. It seems money disappears as fast as I get my hands on it."

Sofia was too preoccupied at the time to pay much attention to Chandler's last few words.

Chapter Nine

The day would be cloudy, but the forecast for the weekend was sunny and beautiful. Sofia was having breakfast and listening to the morning news on the radio. Politics didn't interest her, but she listened to commercial radio daily, so she heard brief bits of the news in between songs. That was enough for her. Today, there was an item about returning vacationers in massive traffic jams.

She hadn't seen him the previous evening. He had gone out early that morning and it must have been very late when he returned. She was thinking about Chandler, and worried about him.

There was no trace of any of him. The news on the radio continued. The details of a bank robbery in the suburbs were given. Three armed, masked men had robbed a bank, making off with approximately three hundred thousand francs. Quite a sizable amount, she thought as the radio announcer went on to say the trio made their getaway in a black car. One witness claimed the first number on the license plate was a seven. According to another, the driver was a man in his late 20s with dark hair, accompanied by a twenty-something blonde woman.

The newscaster droned on for another five minutes or so, and the news, apparently, was all bad.

Depressed, Sofia turned off the radio, finished her coffee and waited for the cleaning lady to arrive before leaving for work. As she entered the front door of the Parlay offices, she ran into Jasper, also on his way to work. She smiled and was about to call out a greeting, but he averted his face and disappeared into the building, quickly moving down the long hallway into his office.

Sofia was surprised and offended. *What a crab!* This was a side of Jasper she had never seen, and she wondered for a moment if anyone ever really knew anyone. Surely Chandler would never have behaved in such a fashion. On the other hand, Jasper wasn't Chandler. Far from it.

Still somewhat shocked and more than a little irritated by Jasper's behavior, Sofia mentioned it to Parlay.

"Don't be too hard on him, Sofia. He's still a long way from being able to accept that you married Chandler. Look here. Some excellent purchase orders have come in this morning. Also, I'd like you to read this letter over and mail it this morning."

That evening, when Sofia returned to the apartment, she traveled part of the way by taxi and the rest on foot. She wanted to take the time to enjoy these last beautiful days of summer. She very much enjoyed playing a stranger in Paris, looking at her surroundings as though they were entirely new to her. It was a game Chandler had taught her. She would discover a picturesque house here, a fountain there . . . and charming little squares she'd never really noticed before.

Chandler—how important he'd become to her. Thanks to him, she was now able to speak English just about perfectly, as fluently as French, and could understand almost everything he was saying, even when he was speaking quickly.

Also, Sofia had dinner in the kitchen, leaving the door to the hallway open—another little trick she'd learned. She hadn't seen Chandler for two days and was hoping he would notice her sitting at the table in the kitchen as he left the apartment. When she heard him come out of his room, her heart began to beat a little faster.

When Chandler appeared in the doorway, she almost choked. Chandler was always well-dressed, but tonight he was in a tux. He wore it with such style! Sofia couldn't remember when he had seemed more fascinating. Her expression of awe brought a smile to his lips.

"Bon appetite, Chandler," she called to him cheerily, "food is now ready. If you can stand my cooking."

Chandler laughed as he sat the table and prepared the wine. Salad and dessert was in the fridge. "Happy to be having such an effect on you, dear," he said, making a greatly exaggerated bow. "I'm on my way to a gala dinner at the Bido, and a black tie is a must."

"You—you are invited to the Bido?" she stammered.

"No. I'm the one who did the inviting. About ten friends." Then more softly, he added, "I'm sorry I couldn't ask you to come along. You would have enjoyed the show too much. But the people I'm going to be with are very sophisticated and I don't think you'd like any of them anyway. You're much too natural. I wish I could tell you how refreshing that is."

Did I just hear what I thought I heard him say? That bastard, how dare he look at me and try to make what I said refreshing. I'm not allowed to be around his friends. Who does he think he is? She was pissed, and not about to stay in tonight.

Even though Sofia was deeply hurt, she couldn't let that show to her handsome stranger-husband. After all, what right did she really have to him? The more she thought about it, the more aggravated she became.

How she was hurting. She would never do such a thing to him. After all the changes she had made, the lies she had told, hiding the truth, and all the people who gave them the gifts at the office party. What a jerk he's become! Now she was wondering if she had made a bad mistake by breaking it off with Jasper. What a fool she felt like.

If she ran Chandler off, she would be without the sex. It was evident it wasn't going to change unless she did something to change it. The biggest reason for her not pulling the plug was the sex.

It must have cost him a fortune to entertain ten guests at the Bido, especially when including a *gala dinner*. He had been complaining about the past few days about being broke. Where had he found so much money so quickly? She pondered the question through her mind's eye all night. She also was going to make him pay for his room. If he could dump on her, what was stopping her from dumping on him?

Sofia eased into his room and placed a note on his pillow explaining that the rent was due and she couldn't accept two weeks. It must be paid in full, and when the month was up, it would be best if he packed his belongings and went back to wherever it was he'd been heading when he was on the train.

Any of this could have been worked out had he not treated her this way. She was the one to make all the changes and couldn't. He was no better.

The next day was Saturday, and Sofia had nothing specific planned. She had done some grocery shopping and went to the library to exchange some books. After lunch, she walked for a while, then went home to write an email to her aunt.

Sofia was still writing when the doorbell rang. She wasn't expecting anyone and was hesitant about opening the door, but the caller was persistent. Slowly, she walked to the hallway. When she heard a man's deep voice asking if this was where a certain Chandler Riggs lived, she was even more perplexed.

As far as Sofia knew, Chandler had never had anyone in

the apartment. And if he had invited someone to come over, surely, he would have warned her ahead of time, if only to ask if it was all right. In many ways, Chandler's behavior might have seemed somewhat out of the ordinary, but at least, until now, his manners had been impeccable.

Sofia's reluctance to open the door must have annoyed the caller, because he rang again and called, "Open up, please. This is the police!"

The word *police* sent shivers up and down her spine. *My God! What had Chandler been up to?* She flung open the door and was faced with a rather impressive-looking, strong-featured man. When he saw her, he smiled.

"Pardon me, Madame," he said. "But it seemed to be taking you a long time to answer the door, and the word *police* almost always does the trick. I wasn't joking, by the way. Here's my identification. May I see Monsieur Riggs?"

"Of course," answered Sofia, her voice trembling. "Please, follow me."

Sofia went to Chandler's door and knocked.

"Someone from the police department is here to see you," she called.

"Ah!" Chandler answered, as though not particularly surprised. "Ask him in."

The man entered the room and closed the door behind him. Sofia only had time to hear Chandler ask the policeman to *have a seat.*

She had too much to think about. Sofia would have liked to have heard what went on, but she wasn't given to eavesdropping at doors. She returned to her room and plummeted into her favorite chair. It was pointless to try to finish the letter to her aunt. She would never be able to concentrate now.

Sofia's heart was pounding. Some of the things Amanda had said were coming back to haunt her. *There's no one worse than the Adonis type for making promises . . . all men are crooks . . .*

No! Chandler couldn't be a criminal. Yet . . . she remembered his own words. At the time, they had seemed of little importance, but now in a different context, they took on a terrible meaning. *A man without a penny to his name and no valid job. Money disappears as fast as I get my hands on it. There are a thousand ways of getting money in Paris.*

How could she be so sure? It wasn't that easy to obtain money if you were earning it, but what if you were stealing it?

The thought shook Sofia to the core. Was Chandler a bank robber? Not a petty thief, but a sophisticated, highly organized criminal? And all that time he spent in his room. Was he drawing up plans of villas, so they could be broken into when their owners were away? What about that bank robbery last Thursday? Chandler had been away all that day.

Sofia tried to remember what she had heard on the radio. The bank robbers had worn masks. The car was a black car, she remembered, like Chandler's. The first number on the Paris license plate had been a seven—like Chandler's, and the driver had been a dark-headed man, like Chandler, with a blonde in the car. That part she wasn't sure about.

Suddenly fear clutched at Sofia's heart. Her whole world was falling apart inside of her. Scarcely breathing, she sat in the chair, motionless, sick to her stomach. *But, how could he?* Surely this wasn't what it appeared to be. Lots of people fit those descriptions. She was trying hard to convince herself that Chandler couldn't have been a part of that robbery. But everything the police said described him to a T.

Then Sofia heard men's voices and heavy footsteps. Chandler was accompanying the officer to the door. She felt an enormous surge of relief as she heard Chandler walk back to his room.

Sofia leaped up from her chair and went into her room without uttering a word to either man. The more she thought about what happened, the more upsetting it was getting. She quickly changed her mind and went straight for Chandler.

"Chandler!" she shouted. "What the hell is going on? And I want the truth, not some lame excuse," Sofia shouted angrily, her expression showing she meant business.

Chandler came out of his room and looked at her, obviously quite taken aback by her apparent distress. "What's the matter? Do policemen always have that effect on you?"

"Have an effect on me? I want to know what is going on and now!" she demanded. "I asked you, what did the police want with you?"

"Nothing that would interest you, dear. He was very nice."

"You can tell that shit to someone else. I knew better than to be nice to you that night on the train. But no, I let you in and you not only got in on my berth, but my heart as well. How could I have been so stupid?" She screamed.

"Sofia, I didn't—" He stopped, speechless.

"Just go, now, before this gets any worse." She finished with tears flowing as she slammed then locked her door to her room.

"You'll have to excuse me. I must leave for Milan right away."

Sofia looked at herself in astonishment. "You're going away? Right now? Abroad?"

"That's right. I guess you could say I'm going abroad. You seem to have a firm grasp of geography, anyway. Sorry to have to rush like this, but I haven't much time."

"Imagine that, it's what people do when they're running from the law."

"I don't tell you everything, do I?"

Sofia shouted, "As a matter of fact, you don't tell me anything! And I've admired you so much, even loved you." But she thought Chandler had already left.

Sofia went to his door, but didn't make any effort to go inside. Suddenly Sofia realized she had broken the cardinal rule—she was in love. How could such a thing happen? She stood still, almost in a trance. She wanted to tell him not to bother coming back.

"How could I let this happen? He has my heart and left with it! Bastard, I'll never let this happen to me again, and will never, ever, allow this again." She cried tears of sorrow, and, pulling herself together, she grabbed a jacket, her purse, and left for a friend's place.

Sofia knew he was involved in a bank robbery. Had she given him the chance to explain, she wouldn't have believed him. He had been ready with all the right answers, as usual, when the police had called, so he hadn't been arrested, but there was no way he'd be able to keep it up. No, the only thing he could do now was run. Put a border between himself and the police.

He was running away—leaving her! No explanations. Not even an attempt to justify himself.

How would Sofia explain Chandler's sudden departure? She realized then her teeth were chattering. She was contemplating whether to call the police or not. She found herself blindly looking out the window, into the night, her eyes full of tears, as if to see Chandler pulling up. What would she do? What would she say if the police came back? A horrible thought occurred to her. What if they accused her of being his accomplice?

If accused, how could she defend herself? A young blonde . . . that was the description of the person sitting next to the driver of the getaway car, and it matched *her*. In a moment of panic, she struggled to keep her composure. Oh, why had Chandler abandoned her? To make matters worse, she'd been late for work the day of the robbery, Thursday morning, and everybody at the office could bear witness to it. If accused, she had no money to hire a lawyer.

A blonde woman and dark-headed man. The police detective had seen her when she opened the door. No doubt he would put two and two together. Both she and Chandler fitted the description perfectly.

Sofia had to get out of her apartment! She would join Chandler in Milan, not just for her own sake but for his, as well. Even if he was guilty, she would not desert him. She couldn't let him continue in a life of crime, when there was still something she could do to help. He had decent feelings. He was not an insensitive man. He had proven that with Frances and Lynn. He was sophisticated and loved beauty in all its various forms. It could only have been his acquaintances, together with his taste for luxury, that had led him into such a crime. It wasn't too late to help him.

Fired by renewed hope, Sofia called a travel agency. She would show him what he had done was wrong and help bring him back to his senses. And everything he had given her in joy and pleasure, she would give back to him in loyalty. His role in the bank robbery had been a minor one. If he agreed to come back to Paris, return the stolen money, and turn in the others who had been his undoing, surely a good lawyer would be able to keep him out of prison.

The next plane for Milan left the following morning and the flight wasn't that long. That would give her most of Sunday morning and all afternoon to search for him. And if it took longer than that to find him, she would rent a hotel room and stay the night.

Without hesitation, she booked the flight. Money was tight, but she had been putting money aside for almost a year.

Right now, only one thing was of any interest to her was to never again hear a man's voice shouting *police* from outside her apartment door.

Sofia hastily packed a few things in a small overnight bag, plus her ID and wallet. Then, because she had to call upon her innermost resources for support in this time of need, she reverted to her former practicality, and had a bite to eat before trying to sleep.

Chapter Ten

At the Milan airport, she hired a taxi and instructed the driver to take her to Cathedral Square. This was the first time Sofia had ever traveled by plane, and she would have enjoyed it thoroughly had her mind not been in such a turmoil. Was she doing the right thing? Was it too much? Was she stalking him? What had she turned into? So many questions with no answers.

At the Milan airport, she had changed her money into Italian currency, In the next moment, the taxi pulled up in front of a beautiful old cathedral. Sofia couldn't speak, let alone understand, a word of Italian, and she wondered if the driver had understood her enough to help. At any rate, she kept repeating the word, *Duomo,* the name of a large square in the center of Milan. She felt reassured when the car turned into a wide avenue.

Sofia knew exactly what she was going to do. The only way to find Chandler was to call all the hotels he might be staying at. Knowing him, it would surely be a luxury hotel, and before leaving Paris, she had asked for the names and numbers of the best hotels in Milan. All she had to do now was to keep calling until she found him.

He had said often enough he was a world traveler. Her task was made a little easier by the hotel phone operators, all of whom spoke either French or English. But time after time, when she asked for Chandler Riggs, the reply was the same, "We have no one here by that name." She had been so sure of finding Chandler this way that she felt quite desperate after she had dialed the last number on the list and still hadn't found him.

There were hundreds of less expensive hotels in Milan and she couldn't possibly call each one. Besides, it was quite possible that Chandler was hiding out in a friend's flat. He had friends everywhere. On the other hand, he could have decided to go elsewhere—Rome, perhaps. And there was always the possibility he had lied to her and gone to Switzerland, or England, or Denmark, or any other country.

She'd worry about Parlay's reaction to her absence later. Although she was completely at a loss as to what to do next, a faint ray of hope still kindled within her. She made up her mind that Chandler was in Milan and not staying with friends. Having decided that much, she told herself she would go to every single hotel in the city, walk up and down every street, even if it took her a week.

Besides, what on earth would Parlay think of her if she went into work and said Chandler had just up and left her after only a short time of marriage? Well, that was the plan, wasn't it? And now, without warning, Chandler was carrying it out!

One particularly eager young Italian tried to stop her in the street. Quite definite now in her plan of action, she began walking. Leaving Piazza Docusio, she took the first street she came to. The men weren't at all embarrassed about staring at her. She knew she made a pleasing picture in her stylish cream-colored dress, and some made complimentary and some not-so-complimentary remarks as she passed. "Where are you going, *Bella Signorina?* Is there any way I can help you?"

Sofia, in her distress, pushed past him aside so violently he almost lost his balance. She mumbled an apology and hurried on.

She felt her spirits drop. She walked quickly, searching

for hotels, and soon found herself back at the large Cathedral Square, having made only two inquiries, both unsuccessful. Already frustrated, she stopped in the cathedral doorway and took a deep breath. For the first time, she became aware of the beauty of her surroundings and the splendor of the great white cathedral, which had recently been sandblasted.

Soon she realized Mass was being celebrated.

Entering the ancient edifice, she was somewhat overwhelmed by the vastness of its interior, which was without pews. She stood just inside the great doors, allowing the feelings of awe to wash over her for a few minutes. and for a while lost her terrible sense of loneliness. "I will never see anything more beautiful than this," she murmured.

It was a large, glass, domed area, and to avoid any men who might try to get her attention, she started to walk around. Sofia emerged from the church feeling much better, only to discover it was raining, people scurrying everywhere for cover. Sofia was sure the downpour wouldn't last, because overhead most of the sky was blue. However, she hadn't anticipated rain and had brought neither raincoat nor umbrella with her. She looked quickly around for shelter. On her right, she noticed a large arcade where several people had gathered to wait out the shower. She hurried toward it.

The whole atmosphere of the place was one of distinct elegance. On both sides of the arcade were shops and numerous restaurants. She had not eaten a thing since breakfast and instinctively stopped to look at a menu posted outside one of the larger restaurants. The list of various pasta dishes made her realize how hungry she really was. Before going in, she peered through the bay window and saw an enormous, beautifully decorated room, filled with small tables, occupied by well-dressed customers. Waiters, dressed in white, moved gracefully among the tables.

Her eyes roamed aimlessly from table to table. Suddenly she jumped. "Chandler!"

There he sat, just a few feet away, on the other side of the bay window. And with him, at the same table, sat a blonde. Both were looking the other way, but Sofia would have known the nape of that neck, the breadth of those shoulders and the particular shade of that dark hair anywhere.

Chandler's accomplice in the holdup was her first thought. The woman turned her head, and Sofia could see her profile. She was stunning, quite young, and dressed like a movie star. Chandler was talking to her as though they were old friends. Sofia just stood, staring, unable to move. *Chandler! And with a blonde.*

They made a stunning couple, she was forced to admit. Sofia, he had left behind in Paris, but not his partner in crime. Of course! What was Sofia to him? Nothing? He must surely be in love with that woman, for how could he help it? She was beautiful. No, not beautiful—she was drop-dead gorgeous.

She was the woman Chandler loved. Sofia felt a burning pain course through her body, a savage, powerless rage. It took her a few moments to realize what was happening to her. Jealousy. How could she help being jealous of that woman?

How naïve could she be? Did she dare make a scene? Maybe Chandler had just taken refuge from the rain with a friend. If she were to walk up to them, her heart on her sleeve, she would only make a fool of herself. And to think she had come here to take him away from his sordid life of crime and help him become a decent man.

"Chandler, my Chandler," she whispered. *Damn you, Chandler.* No, damn *her* for letting herself to be taken in so easily.

So, what if the police came back? Her precious Chandler was gone to the arms of another woman. With great effort, she pulled herself away from the window. She would never have believed that she could hurt so deeply. He was lost to her . . . forever. There was nothing more for her to do in Milan. The trip had been sheer lunacy in the first place. As if he would have been waiting for her. As if she meant nothing to him. Now, there was nothing left to do but return to Paris.

She was sure she'd never allow her heart the much-needed freedom it was going to need. Holding her bag tightly, she started to walk, paying little attention to where she was heading. She arrived at La Scala Square, but even the famous opera house, where the greatest names in the world of music came to perform, didn't interest her. She scarcely noticed the statue of Leonardo da Vinci or the Marino palace. She just kept walking aimlessly, feeling as if she had a knife in her heart.

Sofia turned onto a wide avenue, heedless of where it might take her. She bumped into people, completely unaware of their curious glances. Then, quite suddenly, she stopped. What on earth was the matter with her? Why was she here, wandering about like some drunken fool, in this strange city, over a man of all things? Realizing it was time to put an end to it permanently, she tried to collect her thoughts. It was not likely she would be able to get a seat on the next train headed for home. But surely there would be a night ticket out. She could take a berth and sleep all the way home.

Sofia flagged a taxi and by means of gestures managed to convey that she wished to be taken to the railway station. Once there she learned that a train was leaving for Paris at five. She quickly bought a ticket and went to the coffee shop to wait. She was no longer hungry, but managed to swallow a sandwich and an espresso.

A single beloved name kept repeating itself, over and over, in her heart. On the train, Sofia tried to clear her mind of all her worry and made every effort to think of nothing.

No one there needed to know about her escapade, and providing the police didn't come for her, she could simply return to her old routine. Unable to sleep at all during the night, she arrived in Paris completely exhausted. It was twenty to eight on a bright Monday morning, and she was again in her own, secured world. And in her own heartbreak. She was back in her apartment before the cleaning lady arrived, and at nine she would be at the office.

As she rode the elevator to her floor, she thought about how she had conducted herself all this time. Why hadn't she gone ahead and married Jasper? How could she have allowed herself to be taken in by a stranger, just because he'd been charming and so damned fine?

The feeling that a part of her had just died was overwhelming. Sofia's comfortable apartment seemed hostile now. Throwing down the bag she had been clutching for the past twenty-four hours, she realized she simply didn't know what she was doing any more.

She couldn't go around looking like that. She noticed her reflection in the mirror and was shocked, to say the least. She didn't recognize the person she was staring at. The young woman in the mirror was in a sorry state, with her hair a mess and her clothes wrinkled.

Furious with herself, she cast off her rumpled dress and took a bath, then brushed her hair carefully and put on a pastel pink suit she particularly liked.

In the kitchen, she found a piece of bread and took a bite, only to find it stale. She angrily threw it in the trash. At last she managed to scrounge up few cookies and made herself a cup of hot tea. As she forced herself to eat and drink, her mind was filled with a picture of herself wandering around a strange city where no one knew her and nobody cared. She could visualize the back of Chandler's head and the profile of that beautiful woman with him. Somehow, she couldn't quite believe she was back in Paris, home, in her own apartment, alone, everything screaming *Chandler*. It all had happened in such a short period of time.

At nine o'clock, the cleaning woman arrived. She had her own hey to let herself in. Sofia had already cleaned the room Chandler was using, but his effects were gone as well as he. Maybe she wouldn't be too nosey and notice anything.

"My God, Madame Lincoln . . . what has happened to you?"

Sofia felt like screaming, *Don't call me Madame anymore.* She managed to control the urge and instead replied, "Yes, I know I look dreadful. I didn't sleep very well last night, and this morning I'm a wreck. It's nothing much to worry about."

"Well, I think you should go back to bed. No one should have to go to work in that state. Now, what do you want me to do this morning? Is Monsieur Riggs home?"

Such a simple question, but so upsetting at the same time.

"Uh, no . . ." Sofia stammered. "He's away on a business trip."

"Good. I'll just dust his study, then. There can't be much to do in there, because I did a major cleaning last Thursday, while he was out."

Of course, last Thursday had been the day of the robbery. "My God," mumbled Sofia. "I'm not the only one who knows that Chandler was out all day."

"I beg your pardon?" asked the other woman, looking at her curiously.

"Oh, nothing," Sofia replied hastily. "I'm sorry. I was just talking to myself."

"Well, you'd better put on a warm coat," advised the

cleaning lady. "It's quite cool out today, and it looks like its rain for us again."

It had been raining in Milan. Milan . . .had she really been there?

"Thank you, Madame Pye."

Her legs felt like rubber and she decided to take a taxi to work. Parlay was in the office when she arrived. When he saw her, his reaction was much the same as that of the cleaning woman.

"My dear, are you alright? What is the matter?"

"Nothing serious, Parlay. Just a migraine, that's all."

"You shouldn't have come in! Would you like to go home?"

"No," she replied, knowing that would be the worst thing she could do. "I'd rather work . . .keep myself busy."

She didn't want to be reminded, let alone think of Chandler at that time.

She started to work furiously, but was soon making major mistakes by mixing up the files and having to repeat her work until finally Parlay intervened.

"Sofia, I think you'd better go home. Go to bed and call a doctor if you need to. Take a few days, just keep in touch and come back when you're better. I'll get Katie to fill in till you return."

"Yes, I suppose I should. I can't seem to do anything right today. I'm sorry, Mr. Parlay."

Sofia wanted so much to be taken into someone's arms, to be caressed and comforted. She longed for Chandler. If only he wasn't such a liar and a thief, but instead the Chandler of her own foolish imagination.

He was in the arms of another beautiful woman in his crime world.

As soon as she was back in her apartment, she took two aspirins and crawled into bed. What good that was going to do?. The room began to spin, and she felt as though she were going to be sick. Why was she suffering this way for a man who wasn't worth it? The answer made her feel even more miserable. She loved Chandler with all the passion of her years—loved him the way she had always wanted to love someone. But he was so undeserving! Besides, she didn't have him to worry herself over no longer.

"I won't cry," she murmured. "I won't." It just hit her suddenly—she'd felt like a fool this whole time—could she be considered an accessory to the fact? She could go to jail over someone she really didn't know. She immediately burst into tears.

At last she was finally able to get some much-needed sleep. But her sleep was tortured by dreams of Chandler, and of herself running, running, like a woman possessed, up and down a series of wide, unfamiliar streets, calling desperately for the man she loved.

Sofia stayed in her t-shirt, slept whenever she felt like it, and from time to time wandered listlessly about. For nearly two days, Sofia was unable to leave her apartment. She notified Parlay, who kindly advised her to take the week off. The landlady did her shopping for her, and Sofia didn't even bother to dress. Why should she if everyone else was doing her bidding for her?

Chandler had walked into her life, turned it upside down, and just sat back and let it happen, like any fool would. She tried to read but found she couldn't concentrate. How could she be interested in the problems of fictitious characters when she had serious troubles enough of her own? *Damn Chandler! Damn him!*

She knew he wouldn't be back and she would simply have to get used to the idea. Although she tried not to think about Chandler, every time she heard someone moving about in the hallway or the next apartment, she hoped it was him coming back to her. How could she harbor such hope?

Maybe she could do something for herself with the extra space like she'd always planned. Yet she had said nothing definite to anyone about Chandler's departure. She was waiting until she could speak of it casually, and then, at the same time, she would announce the divorce. She would give away all the things he had left behind and rent out the room. But this time it would be to an older woman who would be interested only in accommodation. Or maybe a place to meditate?

In the meantime, she had to get hold of herself, or everyone was going to know there was trouble in paradise. She couldn't just give up on life because she had suffered a shock. So, Chandler had let her down. Lots of other people had been disappointed just as cruelly and they survived. She had to pull herself out of this ridiculous daze. This wasn't Sofia Lincoln.

Chapter Eleven

The next morning, she made a special effort and took a hot, leisurely bath. She brushed her hair for a long time, then painted her nails. And instead of putting on her housecoat, she chose the very expensive dressing gown she had bought to take with her to Nice on a special occasion. But that thought was out of the question now.

At that point, it was about the only joy she could offer herself—and it wasn't enough to fill the emptiness in her heart. It was a beautiful shade of pastel pink, and just seeing her reflection in the mirror boosted her spirits. The gown reached almost to the floor, making her look quite tall, even dignified.

It was tattooed on her brain. She continued to look at herself in the mirror, and soon it was Chandler she was seeing—his eyes, his hair, his hands. The same Chandler who had said, "I wouldn't want to hurt you." The Chandler who had lied. "Usually, married couples kiss each other." And yes . . . the same Chandler who had been sitting contentedly in the restaurant in Milan with another woman! How could he?

Someone else would feel that joy, now someone else loved her Chandler. It was extremely painful to Sofia to think that she would never rest her head on his shoulder, never again feel the warmth of his hug.

An oddly familiar sound jerked her head back to reality. A key was turning in the lock of the apartment door. She suddenly remembered, that in his haste Chandler hadn't returned her key. Had he thrown it away, to be found by someone else?

She was terrified. But surely, if it was a burglar, he would go away as soon as he realized that someone was home. Sofia was trembling and decided to grab her ball bat from behind the door. She intended to use it if someone were breaking in.

She rushed to the door and was about to call out—but stopped speechless. The door opened and there stood Chandler, relaxed and smiling.

"It's you," she breathed angrily. "I ought to put this bat over your head." She hesitated, hatred in her voice. The surprise and sudden emotion proved too much for her. Choking with joy and unable to control herself, she flew into his arms, burying her head in his jacket and sobbing like a child.

"What the—" he stammered, dropping his suitcases.

For a moment, he held her close, then tenderly lifted her face and considered her eyes.

"Sofia," he asked softly, "What is it? Why the tears?"

"I thought you were never coming back to me," she spluttered. "Oh, Chandler!"

He laughed lightly and kissed her hair.

"Good," he said contentedly. "I'm very happy to hear this, my pet. But do you think it would be alright if I came inside? I wasn't expecting such an enthusiastic reception. As you can see, I'm here now."

Chandler gently freed himself and led her to a chair in the living room.

"Come, my pet. You seem to be in quite a state. Sit down and tell me what this is all about."

"I should be asking you that!"

"Before we say anything else, let me see how lovely you are. I've never seen you look more beautiful, your eyes all shiny with tears. And that gown! Were you on your way to a ball or something?"

"Chandler, don't tease me. It's only a nightgown. I haven't been feeling well. I'm the maddest I've ever been with you. I want you to know I'll never forgive you for the way you have treated me. That I hate you for. You think you're too good to introduce me to your friends! I was the one whose life was turned upside down and I'm no good. You can go to hell for it, too. I'm just as good an anyone else, and surprisingly enough, I have feelings, too."

"Not feeling well?" He sounded dubious. "My pet, you look marvelous."

She shook her head obstinately. "That's not working, either. I've been sick . . . and all because of you! How could you, Chandler?"

"Me? Why? What have I done?"

"You know very well what you've done. Don't you play those damn games with me! Aren't you afraid of being arrested?"

"Arrested? What on earth for, Sofia?"

"Of course we are! Look, Chandler, this isn't the time for jokes. I'm very serious!"

"Alright. But I don't have a clue what you're talking about. However, you can be sure of one thing—the police aren't going to arrest me. Not now, not ever. That I can swear to."

"Maybe not today . . . but these things are always found out, you know that. After all, a bank robbery? Three hundred thousand francs is a lot of money!"

"I see. I'm about to be arrested for robbing a bank. Says who?"

"Nobody has come out and just said it, but the way you've been acting is proof enough. Wednesday, you were broke. By Friday, you had money in every pocket. A new car was used in the robbery. The driver was a young man, a young man that fit your description."

"You heard all that on the news?"

"I'm not lying, dickhead. Don't you feel any remorse at all for what you've done?"

"Not a bit, my pet."

"That's great! Armed robbery is a terrible crime!" she cried. "The least you could feel is ashamed of yourself."

He didn't bat an eye as he listened to her.

"Maybe there's some excuse for you. Your mother was on her own when she was raising you, and a working woman can't always look after her children the way she should. And I suppose that if anyone was hungry enough he'd just grab for something to eat, even if it belonged to someone else. You poor dear! You've probably been living by your wits your whole life."

His gaze remained steady as he continued to look at her.

"And what if I have, Sofia?"

His stare made her uncomfortable, but she managed to speak firmly when she answered.

"I'm going to do everything I can to help you. The least you deserve for the sex. Your mother worked hard to give you a good education and you have a lot going for you. There are lots of ways you can earn an honest living."

"You have been very generous, my pet."

"This had nothing to do with generosity! It's very painful for me to see a man like you are, wasting his entire life away."

As she spoke, his face showed not the slightest trace of emotion. What kind of person could break the law, convince a woman to fall in love with them, and fly anywhere they wanted on no money?

Apparently quite unconcerned, Chandler slowly pulled all his pockets inside out, dropping an expensive gold case he carried.

Sofia watched him, unable to drag her eyes away from the expensive case. "Was that stolen, too?"

Suddenly, she became very angry. "I don't seem to be getting through to you, Chandler!"

"Ah, for one, no, it's not stolen. I used to smoke and carried my cigarettes in it, and now I use it for my gum. For two, you are getting through, my pet. Loud and clear."

"Stop it. All you're doing is making this worse, and my nerves can't take it. On top of everything else, you don't seem to realize that you have put me in a very compromising position for a second time. The woman who was with you . . . people will think it was me. I feel like I'm on the verge of a heart attack."

He chewed his gum and looked at her, frowning.

"I see. I had another woman with me that fit your description, did I?"

"Yes, you did, and a beautiful one, too. I saw her in Milan!"

Sofia bit her lip, only then realizing what she had said. Now the damage was done.

"Milan? What were you doing in Milan?"

"I ran away, just like you did, Chandler. I was scared."

Reluctantly, she told him the whole story, including the details of her search that she'd hoped would result in his returning the stolen money.

Chandler listened in silence, pacing the floor. When Sofia finished, he stopped in front of her and gazed into her eyes with great tenderness. "My sweet love," he said softly, "how marvelous to know you would go through so much for me."

Sofia backed off. "Don't call me your sweet love. You love that damn woman, the woman you ran to in Milan. And now you expect to come back here to me? What kind of man does that, Chandler? What kind?"

"Look at you. You're jealous! This is far more than I ever

expected."

"Damn it, Chandler! Stop playing games with me, I'm nowhere near being just upset with you!"

"Then stop being so hard on me, Sofia. I've never been more serious, nor have I ever been happier. Do you really think anyone could live as close to you as I have, for as long as I have, without becoming attached to you?"

For a moment, Sofia weakened. There was no sarcasm in his voice, and his eyes were filled with great tenderness. Surely this man was no criminal. Yet—giving herself a shake, she regained her determination.

"I'm sorry you think so little of me," he said, starting his pacing one again. "And despite that warm reception, I suppose you would like for me to leave right away?"

She didn't answer right away. *Send him away?* That was what she should have done, but did she have the courage? Not today, that much she knew. Lowering her head and very conscious of her own weakness, she murmured, "I've already said I'd do anything I could to help you."

He spun around. "Does that mean I can stay? What a strange little creature you are! Thank you, Sofia, but I don't need your help. You should be glad you're dealing with someone like me. Some day that kind of heart of yours will really get you into trouble."

She didn't answer. She was somewhere deep inside herself, trying to sort out her feelings. Doubt and hope surged alternately through her. He seemed so sincere!

At her silence, he went on, "Stop all this worrying about me, Sofia. Forget this whole crazy obsession. Obviously, you need something to take your mind of it. Let's see . . . do you like sauerkraut? You do? Then I'm inviting you to have some with me tonight."

She looked at him in exasperation. "On the money from the robbery, Chandler?"

"I have not seen a franc from that holdup, my pet, believe me. Now, what do you say? Are we friends or not?"

"I could never be your enemy, Chandler. But on the other hand, I could never be friends with a criminal, either. I've told you, you may stay, but it can only be for a little while. Don't patronize me. I must have time to think about all this. You confuse me so." She started to cry.

Chandler looked at her with concern. "My darling, don't upset yourself this way. Look, we can forget the sauerkraut. We'll have it later, or never, if that's what you want."

He knelt beside her and took a handkerchief from his pocket to dry her tears. "I'm sorry if I've upset you. Come, you'll ruin your lovely eyes. Life is quite beautiful, Sofia. Truly it is . . . you'll see. I'm not a criminal, and everything's going to be all right."

Two tears rolled down Sofia's cheeks. "Chandler! I want so much to believe you."

"Then believe me! There, now. Feeling better?"

She nodded and dropped her head, then looked up again into his eyes.

"You have a lot of nerve, Chandler. Promise me that you'll never again steal anything?"

He smiled. "I promise, my love. I'll never take anything that belongs to someone else." For a long moment, he looked at her. "Happy now?"

"Not really, but I know that doesn't matter much to you. Just keep your word. You think you can do at least that without any issues?"

"I will. I swear on your lovely little hands." At that, he took her hands in his and kissed them.

"I can assure you," he added, "basically I'm quite an honest fellow."

She looked closely at him, suspecting that he was making fun of her again, but she could find only sincerity in his eyes.

"I'm very tired," she mumbled, "and I'd like to be alone for a little while, if you don't mind?"

Sofia would never allow Chandler to walk away from her again. Sofia's eyes gleamed as she confessed. "Are we touched by the same flame, Chandler?" Now she knew real desire. She had tasted him on her lips, felt him with her body, relived it in her mind. She had never known love like this before. With Jasper it was different, nothing like the feeling she shared for Chandler.

Looking at his face was like looking directly into the sun, bringing to her a feeling of absolute warmth and radiance. She put her mouth to his and they kissed until they both trembled and gasped to breathe. His lips left hers and brushed across the side of her face and down her throat.

"You will always come back to me, won't you, Chandler?" she demanded. "Tell me you will always come back to me, that you won't ever leave."

In that moment everything else, everyone else, became meaningless. Chandler's voice restrained by passion, he murmured in response, "Yes, I'll always come back, my pet." His words came from his heart, not his mind. The truth revealed itself in the kiss that followed the words.

"All day I haven't thought of anything but you." They finally made it to the bed in a whirling embrace. Chandler lowered himself toward Sofia, pressing her down until her head lay on the pillow. Gazing at her, into her luminous eyes, he told her in soft words, "I want you so much. I can't think of anything else."

Sofia appeared in her smile. "You have me, Chandler. I'll be yours forever."

Chandler didn't move. He remained motionless, a gentle expression on his face. "I'm in love with you, Sofia."

"Is that so bad?" Sofia rubbed her chin against his cheek.

Chandler's laugh was low, smooth. "*Disastrous* is the

more appropriate word."

Sofia held him captive with her arms, with her mouth, as his lungs labored for air. Opening her mouth, she reached for his lips and they hurled together in a suffocating embrace. She returned his kisses with her whole heart, her whole self. He wove his hands into her hair as she dug her nails through his denim shirt, clinging to him. She didn't want to let him go, not even for an instant. It was really happening. He had said, *I'm so in love with you*, just the way she had dreamed he would. She dared not let him go, for fear he would change his mind.

His mouth invaded hers, wetting her lips, his tongue joining hers in an exquisite pleasure that spun golden blood through her veins. He pulled away and she lay back, watching the precision of his hands as he took off his clothes. Then he lowered himself toward her. Her head arched back into the pillow when she felt his mouth touching her stomach, her body, in swift movements. Both hands were firmly over her breasts, caressing her flesh gently while his mouth plied into the smooth, soft bareness of her body, over and over until her excitement could not be contained.

It was an emotion set aside from all others, completely self-sufficient. She reached for him, long slender fingers gliding along his firm, bare skin. Her desire for him became the strongest sensation she had ever known. In her mind there was nothing ahead of them, nothing behind them. Only the desire of *now*. And desire did not create tomorrows or relive yesterdays.

Sofia's hands were bold and aggressive, seeking the source of his greatest desire, experimenting with a new freedom that almost frightened her.

She wanted to please him as he had pleased her. She wanted to discover everything about him. Chandler didn't mind or stop to scold her, to tell her not to do that, it wasn't fitting. He sighed with enjoyment as Sofia touched him, and that made touching him more pleasurable than anything she had ever done.

Opening her eyes, she marveled to herself at the beauty of his body. She came up to a sitting position, her gaze slowly traveling the length of him, stretched out beside her. She wanted to learn more than his body—she wanted to know the thoughts in his mind. Haltingly she whispered, "What do you think makes these feelings?"

Chandler's mouth hung loosely, his gaze mesmerized on her face. "Passion needs desire," he said breathlessly.

Slowly Chandler raised himself up and took her face in both his hands, bending close to her mouth. "This is the way love feels. All good feelings. There's nothing evil about it." He kissed her passionately.

Sofia's lips quivered, and she felt the shaking start deep inside her. His chest joined hers and she stirred beneath him as his kiss deepened, his tongue darting in and out of her mouth. His kiss hardened, his tongue ran over her teeth and captured hers in a long, savoring curl. A throaty cry escaped her as he sank carefully down, covering her body with his warm flesh. A sense of being alive came to her, filling her with cravings for him. In his arms she was truly at peace with herself, and with the world. This was love, this feeling inside her. Sofia stared at him, a dreamy happiness in her eyes. "It's wonderful, isn't it? Feeling this way?"

Chandler took possession of her then, all of her. She pressed her hands into his back and felt the tenseness of his muscles, the tautness of his body. He was rushing her, but she didn't care. She welcomed it. She welcomed him and the swirling sensation he brought to her. She caught her breath sharply, feeling the chill of flames move up her legs and down her body to meet in a soaring blaze reaching beyond her.

It seemed a strange thing to her that in a time of such intimate closeness, dissolved together, the moment of the greatest ecstasy was experienced alone, as fleeting as a breath of air. When Sofia returned to her body, she was limp and breathless and listening to the soft ringing in her ears. She was barely conscious that he was kissing one shoulder. For a moment she hardly knew he was there beside her. And then she was once again aware of his hands, his mouth, his body.

"What are you thinking right now, this moment?" Sofia looked over at Chandler, lying on his side, his eyes closed. She could see the moistness on his skin from the light shining in from the kitchen. "Chandler," she said lovingly.

Chandler's eyes came open and he gave her a warm, tender smile. "I was thinking about you, and how beautiful you are." Raising up on one elbow, he reached out with one hand and gently pushed the hair back from her face.

The moment was priceless. He didn't need to say a word.

CHAPTER TWELVE

I'm such a fool, she thought, to love him so much. I love him with all my heart.

Sofia returned to work, and there, at least, everything seemed to be going quite well. There were a few problems to iron out, but now she felt strong enough to cope with them.

She had resolved not to go out with Chandler again, and the strength of her willpower surprised even herself. From time to time she saw him in the apartment. He always managed to run into her quite casually, as though it were all very natural and unplanned.

He had resumed his mocking ways, and Sofia, while she still loved him, knew the time was fast approaching when she would have to put an end to their so-called *marriage*.

Undoubtedly, there were other men in the world, and how well Sofia knew this, men who would be honest, who would talk about their past and take pride in their origins and families, men whose plans could be made for the future, men she wouldn't hate and love at the same time. She would never love anyone the way she loved him, but she wanted a home. Her whole life lay ahead of her, time enough to undo the past and start over.

Yes, it was time for her to act. She couldn't go on renting her room to a criminal. And this time, she wouldn't let herself be dissuaded or influenced, as she had been in the past.

"Chandler, I have to talk to you. Please come into the living room."

"Here I am, my pet. My goodness! How serious you look.

Have I committed another robbery?"

"I hope not. You promised never to do it again!"

"The *again* is inaccurate, Sofia. Don't misquote me. What I promised was never to steal. By the way, I have good news for you. Perhaps you've already heard it on the news. The police have arrested the three people who robbed that bank, and part of the money has been recovered."

"What about the man who was driving the car, and the woman sitting beside him?"

"Vanished! And the police aren't going to pursue them — they have too many other things to do."

"But the police came here to question you."

"That was just a friendly visit, my pet. There was nothing special about it."

"You always seem to have an answer for everything, Chandler, but even you have to admit that sometimes coincidence can lead to confusion. Why won't you tell me what you were doing Thursday?"

"Why don't we drop all this unpleasantness and you can tell what it was you wanted to see me about?" Chandler looked at her with a twinkle in his eye. "Forgive me, my pet. I didn't realize that a make-believe husband was supposed to tell his make-believe wife everything. All you must know is that I have a very good alibi, and furthermore, I've never been involved in anything like that in my life."

She hesitated. Away from him, she could convince herself she would be strong. But near him . . . she could feel herself wavering. Still, she had too much pride not to follow through with what she had intended.

She lifted her head and spoke as coldly as she could. "Yes, Chandler, I wanted to tell you I will be needing your room soon. I'm going to rent it out to an older woman."

He didn't seem particularly surprised. "But, Sofia, you'll be bored to tears. Think of all the fun you have with me."

His eyes twinkled. "Haven't you noticed that there's never a dull moment when I'm around? Why, I'm positively fascinating, if I do say so myself. When we were going out together, life was much more pleasant for you — at least, I hope it was — and didn't I do you a great favor by saving you from that dreadful Jasper you were planning to marry? However, if you insist on being ungrateful and coldhearted, I guess there's nothing I can do about it. I'll just have to leave."

She stared right into his eyes. "I'm not ungrateful. And I'm anything but coldhearted."

"An alcoholic, perhaps? A woman chaser? Good for you! And I hope you believe in happiness, too. People keep chasing after it, so it must exist. The secret is, of course, to grab hold of it when it comes your way. All modesty aside, aren't you happy with me living here, sharing your apartment? Why do you want me to leave? I would be miserable away from you, and you'd be miserable anywhere but with me. And what would I become without you?"

He smiled at her, and she stamped her foot in exasperation. "But we can't go on like this forever," she cried angrily. "I want to get married someday."

"I do, too. What a marvelous idea! Let's get married to each other."

"Chandler!" she stammered in dismay. Her dismay grew even greater as she realized that Chandler was speaking out in earnest. She blushed, trying to speak, but couldn't utter a sound.

"Now don't get carried away. It's really quite simple," he continued. "Everyone we know thinks we're already married. All we need is a simple ceremony and a piece of paper to make it legal. See?"

She remained silent.

"You were complaining earlier about never knowing what I'm doing, so you can see the advantage to being married. No more secrets, no mystery, no more talk about holdups, or bank robberies. Just one big, beautiful understanding. Unless," he added mockingly, "you'd rather marry that Jasper fellow."

"Oh, no!" she blurted. "Jasper definitely isn't the man for me. But he isn't the only man in the world . . . and neither are you."

"And I can't for the life of me see any good reason why you wouldn't want to marry me. I know, and because you're so beautiful, it wouldn't take long for you to find just how many others there are. Women like you are very rare. You know when to be serious and when to have fun. You can be restrained while at the same time quite daring. In a word, you're priceless. One thing I can promise you, Sofia, with me, you'll never be bored."

Neither could she. Except . . . what would she really be letting herself in for? She tried once more to resist the overwhelming influence this man had over her. She lifted her head and looked at him defiantly.

"You told me once that marriage didn't appeal to you."

"I've changed my mind. I've decided that marriage isn't all that bad. And with you, I think I could be an ideal husband. Come on, Sofia. Be optimistic. Sooner or later, you'll see I have a lot of good points."

Still, she continued to test him. Trust him, love him? . "Perhaps you think I'm rich. If you do, you'll find you're very much mistaken."

"The thought never entered my mind. I want to marry you because I love you, not whether you have money or not." He looked at her tenderly, his voice soft. Gently, he took Sofia's hands and pulled her toward him. She trembled as he caressed her arms.

"No, Chandler," she protested, feeling herself weakening. She rested against him as he continued to speak in a tone she had never heard before.

"I love you, and I can't imagine life without you. Can you see yourself spending the rest of your life with any other man? Living with someone else every day, morning till night? Especially the nights, Sofia?"

She shivered. Yes, she had to agree. Lifting her head, she said in a small voice, "Do you really want to marry me, Chandler?"

He kissed her hair. "Yes, I do," he said forcefully. "I'm very sure . . . and this time it will be for real, with a priest, in front of the mayor, in front of the whole world, if that's the way you'd like it. At first, because of the way we met, I suppose staying with you was just another adventure, a new kind of game, but now I'm madly in love with you, and I think you feel the same way about me, Sofia."

"Yes, I do love you," she murmured in reply, voicing her feelings at last.

"Then, my love, why do you resist this beautiful thing between us?"

"Because I'm afraid, Chandler. I don't know anything about you." She considered his eyes. "Who are you?"

He smiled. "A charming, handsome man. Isn't that enough?"

"Enough to make me laugh, to break my heart, but not enough to be the father of my children."

"How would you know?"

"You keep so many things from me."

"Yes . . . but it's so unfair of you to ask me to do this. True, I'm asking you to have confidence in me to the very end, Sofia. That would be proof that you really love me. Do you think you can?"

She hesitated for a moment, but she was now beyond the point where she could think logically. Her feelings were in complete control of her mind. Perhaps she would never be completely happy with Chandler, but without him life would be unbearable.

"But you did say yes, my pet."

The very fact that she belonged to Chandler, whoever or whatever he was, seemed to her the greatest reason for happiness she had ever known. Holding her close, he kissed her forehead, her eyes, and then her lips. Unable to resist any longer, Sofia abandoned all effort at thought and closed her eyes. She had agreed to marry a man she didn't know. She no longer asked herself whether he was honorable. The love she felt was much too powerful, but at the same time incredibly gentle.

She realized, however, that with him, life would always be in turmoil, maybe even dangerous sometimes, and always complicated. But she didn't care. She agreed to place her confidence in him. If she was behaving as though she was under a spell, it was because she was a woman very much in love. And very happy.

CHAPTER THIRTEEN

That night they went out for a nice dinner and Chandler ordered champagne.

"We must celebrate, my love. Is it alright if I call you *my love*? I've wanted to for such a long time. This is our engagement night. A real engagement, this time, and it's only the beginning. You're going to leave that dreadful job of yours."

"It's not dreadful, Chandler," she interrupted.

"Sorry, my pet, but you will leave that job of yours. See how easy I am to get along with?"

"If I don't work, Chandler, what will we live on?"

"Leave that to me, my pet . . . and I won't have to steal, I swear. In any case, I don't want you going back to that office where you're likely to run into Jasper. I'm jealous, you see, terribly jealous. I want you all to myself, Sofia. All of you."

"Very well. I'll leave. Then what?"

"We'll go to England and you can meet my mother. Then we'll get married there as soon as we can. I've waited long enough."

She didn't answer. Until now, he had said very little about his mother. As far as she knew, or imagined, his mother was the widow of a man who had to provide her living in a run-down neighborhood, weary of her life of work and worry.

"Won't we inconvenience your mother if we just drop in on her?" she asked.

"Not at all. Quite the contrary, in fact. She'll be delighted to meet you."

Sofia wasn't so sure. At any rate, she made up her mind to try her best to like Chandler's mother and, if possible, love her.

"You don't seem too overjoyed, my love."

"Of course, I am!"

"Is there something wrong with the sweetbreads, or perhaps you don't like the mushroom sauce?"

"Everything is delicious, Chandler, and . . . I'm looking forward to meeting your mother."

"More champagne?"

"No, thank you. I'm not used to it, you know."

"I love to travel. Is that all right with you?" He laughed.

It was true she felt a little intoxicated, but there was no way of knowing whether it wasn't too agreeable.

"We'll spend our winters in Paris or Rome. Or perhaps Egypt. It's time you did some traveling, saw something of this big old world we live in."

"How could I object to such plans? It sounds fantastic. If only it could be possible . . ."

"But it can be, my love. You'll see. I have all sorts of surprises for you."

Of that, she had no doubt. She only hoped that some of the surprises would be pleasant. As Chandler eyed her mischievously, she realized that his smile always fascinated her, even when it upset her.

The power of love, she thought to herself. How many mistakes were made in its name?

The next morning Sofia got ready as usual, but this day was different—she was turning in her notice. Hard as it was going to be, she was hoping Parlay would understand. She unlocked the door and was always as usual the first one there.

"I need to speak with you, Parlay, I have something that I need to discuss."

"Sofia, you can't do this to me, I know what you're getting ready to say to me," cried Parlay. Sofia had just given her resignation notice.

"I'm so sorry, too, really I am," she replied. "But my husband . . ." She found it easier to say the word now that it was closer to the truth. "He doesn't want me working any more, Parlay. I can't say that I agree with him completely, but in any case, we're going to England, so I can meet his mother. Chandler is very anxious for me to meet her, and I can understand that."

"I quite agree, dear. But couldn't you take a month's leave of absence, instead? Listen, don't make a definite decision right now. I'm not suggesting you go against your husband's wishes, but usually, both husband and wife work during the first years of marriage, if only to save a little money for the children who come later."

Just one of the many differences between the two that made life with Chandler much more exciting than it could have ever been with Jasper. It occurred to Sofia that Jasper would have never thought of that. Traditional, practical even, to save for future children. But Chandler wasn't the type to concern himself with practicalities.

"We also plan to do some traveling. We're going to Rome, and later to Egypt."

Parlay stared at Sofia in shock. "Your husband must be very wealthy. Unless, of course, he expects to be traveling on business."

Chandler didn't have any kind of business, or at least that she knew of. In fact, he didn't seem to have much of anything. And that was what scared her the most, promise or no promise.

"Everything is very much in the planning stage right

now," she mumbled.

"I see. Well then, you must write me from England and let me know what you've decided to do. Meanwhile, consider yourself still an employee of this firm."

"My goodness, Mr. Parlay, that's so wonderful of you to do that for me," she cried. "I don't know anyone who'd do that just for me. Thank you!" She paused. *Maybe I will need this job in a month.*

"Becky could take my place for a while," suggested Sofia.

"Becky isn't as knowledgeable as you for this job, Sofia, by any means."

"But she'll get the hang of it quick, trust me. She's very bright."

"I'm sure she is, but, she's not you. My dear, I've known you since you were a little girl. You are like part of my family, as you well know."

"Yes, and I thank you. You've been very good to me and I'm very grateful." Tears filled her eyes. "Oh! I really am sorry for leaving," she continued. "But perhaps when I come back, I can work part-time. I really can't see myself sitting at home doing nothing."

"You certainly would be bored, since you're so accustomed to activity. However, this is something you and your husband must settle. In any event, you will always be welcome here. Now off with you, with my blessings . . . and have a good life."

She still knew very little about Chandler. Sofia had never been outside continental Europe, and traveling to England was quite an event. Thanks to Chandler and their English conversations together, she had been able to polish her accent. From the standpoint of language, he had foreseen everything.

On the eve of their departure, he came into the apartment,

bursting with enthusiasm. "Here you are, my love. Two plane tickets to Bristol."

She stared at him in puzzlement.

"Flight time—an hour and a half. A mere nothing," he went on.

She looked at the tickets, then back at Chandler.

"Bristol? I was under the impression your mother lived in London."

"Not everybody in England lives in London, my pet."

Once she was in England, she'd be trapped, and it would be very difficult to do anything but to accept things as they were—modest and pitiful though they might be. She was annoyed, but realizing he wasn't about to elaborate, she turned away. Why was he leaving it to her to find out everything for herself? Was he afraid that if he told her the truth she wouldn't go? He'd asked her to have confidence in him, Sofia thought, but he didn't seem to have any inclination to trust her. Was the truth so dreadful?

In a state of joy, mixed with apprehension, she began to pack her suitcase. She was surprised at herself for being able to love him so much that she had given in to his every whim. She knew she would never be able to lead Chandler around by the nose, but nevertheless, going to another country to marry a man she knew nothing about was foolish, if not downright dangerous. Just the same, she had been free to choose between being prudent and gambling on adventure.

The most important thing was pleasing her future husband. What should she take? Judging from the ups and downs of Chandler's previous finances, she had gathered that he came from anything but a wealthy family. Perhaps it would be better to take only simple clothes. But on the other hand, Chandler was always very dressed, and he liked her to look elegant. That settled it. Too bad if her clothes were a little beyond the humble environment of his mother's home.

She packed all her finery—lingerie, daytime and evening dresses, coats, jewelry . . . and to wear on the trip, she chose a new cherry red suit.

When Chandler saw her in it, he let out a wolf whistle. "You look adorable, darling. What a stunning wife I'm going to have. I'll have to keep my eye on you in case someone tries to steal you away."

Would she be able to adapt to the English way of life? Sofia had little time to think during the flight. Determined to please her in every way, Chandler did everything to keep her amused and relaxed, but at the same time he managed to avoid answering any questions. Despite all his efforts to distract her, Sofia couldn't help feeling a little worried. What would she find in England? Would she be welcomed? Would she get along with Chandler's mother? When the plane was almost ready to land, Chandler looked at Sofia with a strange expression.

"I know, darling, that I've caused you a lot of worry. But soon there will be no more secrets. I wish I could tell you how happy I am."

Sofia didn't answer. She wished that she, too, could be equally happy, but anxiety was interfering. Her heart was starting to beat faster.

Chandler was well-known at the airport and they were cleared through customs in no time. As soon as they were through, he took Sofia by the arm and steered her outside.

"My mother has sent her car for us. You'll meet old reliable Jessy soon enough. Not only is he an excellent chauffeur, but he's a fine gardener, as well."

Chandler guided her toward a shiny black Rolls. Beside it stood a chauffeur in full uniform. Sofia's eyes widened in surprise—she'd wondered if perhaps he meant an old beat-up car and a gardener dressed in grubby work clothes.

The man tipped his hat and greeted Chandler in very proper English. "Good day, Mr. Riggs," he said respectfully. Then turning to Sofia, he added, "And very best wishes to you, miss." The man was clearly trying to maintain an expression of indifference, but his eyes sparkled with pleasure.

Too surprised to answer, Sofia just nodded respectfully, while Chandler touched the man on the shoulder in a friendly gesture.

"Thank you, Jessy," he said. "This is Sofia Lincoln, my fiancée. Jessy, I see your health is excellent as usual. Is everything all right at the house?"

"Yes, sir, and Mrs. Riggs is most delighted." He opened the rear door and Chandler and Sofia walked around the car to get in.

"You didn't tell me —"

"Shush, my pet. I know I didn't tell you anything. I asked you to trust me, remember? I hope you won't be sorry you said yes."

By this point, Sofia had no idea of what to think. It was useless trying to question Chandler. Judging by the road signs, the car was not taking them to Bristol. She asked him where his mother had lived.

"My mother lives in Bath. I thought you knew."

How could she know? He hadn't told her anything about his mother, or anyone else in his family. What was more, he knew he hadn't.

"My grandmother lives in Bristol," he went on. "We'll visit her another day. My sister lives in London with her husband and children. I also have any number of cousins all over England. You're marrying into a very large family, and they're all dying to meet you. But my mother wanted to be first."

If he hadn't been so secretive and mysterious, Sofia might

have been able to relax. But she had come here expecting the worst, and it wasn't long before she started imagining Chandler's family. The spotless Rolls and the impeccable Jessy didn't necessarily mean a thing. Both could have been borrowed from Mrs. Riggs' employer for the occasion.

Sofia was holding her breath, when Chandler noticed her anxiety and gently took one of her hands in his. "Stop worrying, my darling. I'm right beside you the entire time, ready to protect you from all the evil. Look around. You'll see all the beauties of England. I must admit I love it here. And I'm so happy to have you here with me."

Sofia turned to look out the window. The sky was overcast, and the temperature was a little cooler that it had been in Paris, but the countryside was a beautiful green, much like the green of springtime, even though it was now almost the end of September.

"The Bath countryside is quite extraordinary," enthused Chandler. "If you like old castles, I'll take you up north to Scotland, where there are lots of them, including a few that are reported to be haunted."

"Haunted? Really?" Sofia was greatly surprised.

"Oh, yes. The British are very fond of their ghosts and don't like the idea of them moving off. It's one of our best-known characteristics. Unfortunately, our house in Bath doesn't have any."

"Well, I don't think that's anything to be sorry about. I'd be petrified if I ever ran into one." Sofia shuddered with slight fear. She didn't get along with ghosts and didn't want to take one home with her, either.

"But most of them are charming. Sometimes they can be a little too playful, mind you, but the people who live with them consider them as part of the family. Just imagine, they've been roaming the hidden passageways and cellars of some of these places for centuries!"

"How many secret passageways and cellars are there in your house?" asked Sofia, not without alarm.

"Not a one." Chandler sighed. "The house has been completely renovated, and if there ever were any, they're gone now. Besides, my mother is very much like you. She would be most upset to find a ghost living in her house, although I'm sure she wouldn't take very long to establish rapport. She can get along with anybody."

Sofia didn't persist with her questioning. She remembered once reading about a haunted castle in an intriguing novel . . . but that had just been fiction.

CHAPTER FOURTEEN

They were on the road from Bristol to London, and in both directions, the traffic was quite heavy. Bath was a renowned resort city that attracted people from all over, even now in the off-season.

As a result, it was quite some time before they reached Bath, although the distance from Bristol wasn't that great. Sofia noticed that, as well as driving on the left, the cars traveled a lot slower than what she was accustomed to. No one seemed in any hurry to get anywhere, not to mention no one was making any effort to pass. Each car just rolled along casually—very unlike the French.

Finally, the car turned off the main road onto a residential street of stunning mansions and parkland. The car slowed as they approached an enormous wrought-iron gate which had been left open. At the end of the driveway stood a large red brick Tudor house. In front of the house was an immaculately tended lawn, divided by a walkway and bordered with wide beds of multicolored flowers.

As the car started up the driveway, Sofia turned to Chandler in surprise. "Where are we going?"

"This is where I live, darling," he answered, with a wink of amusement. "Or perhaps I should say, this is my mother's place, where I used to live."

Chandler put a restraining hand on her arm. Two Irish setters were playfully rolling on the lawn. At the sound of the approaching car, they stopped their antics and, barking with joy, rushed over. As the car came to a stop, Sofia instinctively reached to open the door herself, but Chandler stopped her.

"Don't, my dear. If you were to get out of the car without his help, Jessy would have a heart attack!"

Sofia waited as Jessy walked around the car, hat in hand, and opened the door.

The two setters began jumping up and down all over Chandler, then, curious, stopped long enough to sniff Sofia's skirt, before returning to their master.

"Are they . . . yours, Chandler?" asked Sofia, more and more confused.

"They are, indeed," he gasped, battling to control the dogs' enthusiastic show of affection. "And they seem to be trying to prove it. Okay, boys, settle down. Come, Star, come Beauty! That's enough."

Gently pushing the animals aside, he turned toward the veranda, where a young looking woman with brown hair waited to greet them.

"And this, my dear Sofia, this is my mother," he said proudly. *His mother!*

They moved with the same ease and their eyes bore the same lively expression. Were it not for a few lines in the woman's face, they could easily have been mistaken for brother and sister. All the things Sofia had imagined, for what little Chandler had told her about his mother, raced through her mind—the two dank rooms in the basement of a dilapidated building in some London slum, the old widow in shabby clothes, worn out by life's hardships . . . but now . . . now, she was seeing a smartly-dressed, attractive woman, who was certainly far from old. She wore a beautiful skirt and matching sweater, and around her neck was a delicate necklace, a fine chain of gold from which hung an exquisite amber. Without a doubt, it was from her that Chandler got his charm, his short, straight nose, and firm, gentle lips. Only the color of their hair was different.

So this is Chandler's mother, thought Sofia, thoroughly confused, and this is his mother's home! Only her deep sense of personal pride prevented Sofia from losing her composure. Chandler had put his arm around her shoulders and was introducing her to his mother.

"Mother, I want you to meet the woman I love!" Chandler was amazingly glowing with Sofia on his arm.

"Congratulations, Chandler. She is absolutely lovely . . . but, come children, let's go inside . . . yes, the dogs, too."

Sofia's consternation and embarrassment didn't escape the notice of Mrs. Riggs. Nonetheless, being very kind, as well as blessed with the ability to handle almost any situation on the spur of the moment, she replied cordially, "I'm delighted to meet you, Sofia. I've been waiting a long time for this day. May I say I don't believe my son could possibility have made a better choice."

Everything was spotless and arranged to give the feeling of comfort and security. The décor of the living room was a delicate symphony of shades of green. The furniture was what Sofia considered to be very English, all period pieces, and the carpets were deep and soft. Vases of fresh-cut flowers added just the right touch and made the whole room bright and cheerful.

"I hope the flight hasn't tired you too much?" said Mrs. Riggs, intent on making Sofia feel right at home.

"Oh, no, not at all," murmured Sofia, not yet fully recovered. "But I do feel a little confused. Everything's so different here."

Chandler's mother smiled. "I know just how you feel. I felt the same way when my husband brought me to England from France for the first time. Please sit down, dear. We'll have tea shortly—I'm sure we could all use a cup. Your arrival is quite a special occasion . . . and a very happy one for the whole household."

She looked at Chandler with an air of respect and glanced quickly at Sofia as she drew the table toward them. The door opened and a rather stout woman, dressed in black and white, pushed a serving table into the room. On it was a magnificent silver tea service. "Tea is served," she announced, as though taking part in a sacred ritual.

"Thank you, Mrs. Banes," replied Chandler's mother, in the same ceremonious tone. The two setters, until now seated quietly at their master's feet, began to wag their tails and sniff at the serving table.

"I believe I'd better take them," said Mrs. Banes. "They'll just make a nuisance of themselves in here."

"I suppose you're right." Chandler sighed. "Star, Beauty! Out you go!" The big, red setters with their bright, flowing red manes were gorgeous and both well-behaved. Chandler loved them. He motioned for both dogs to go back out again. Chandler had been around them since his mother bought them.

Looking very woeful, the dogs left the room. Mrs. Riggs followed them and closed the door quietly behind her. "Lord," said Chandler, getting up from his chair, "Mrs. Banes is always so formal. I wonder what she'd do if I jumped into her arms like I used to do when I was a boy, coming home from school. Have a stroke probably . . . never mind. God knows we love each other, and we all know that English servants live by the old traditions. Fortunately, mother and I . . ." His voice trailed off as mother and son looked at each other and started to laugh.

"Yes," said Mrs. Riggs, starting to pour the tea, "we like things to be a little more casual. I'm not too particular about etiquette. Just the same, I'm very lucky to have been able to keep good people so long currently, when it's almost impossible to find good people . . . milk, Sofia? Sugar? Have a roll.

"Mrs. Banes is Jessy's wife, and they've been with me since my children were very young—years and years. Help yourself, Chandler. I also have a woman who comes in every morning to clean the house. It's much too large now, of course, but all my memories are here, and Bath is such a love city. In June, at festival time, there are some excellent shows and the countryside is so delightful . . . . but then, I'm sure Chandler has told you all about it."

Sofia was about to say that Chandler hadn't told her about anything, but Mrs. Riggs had turned to her son and was continuing.

"I don't doubt that you've enjoyed your stay in Paris, since you've come home with this delightful young woman, Chandler. I also hope that you've been able to get some work done."

Sofia started. *Work? Chandler? Not likely!* She looked at him, expecting to see embarrassment, but as usual, he was totally at ease. Sofia could feel her insides twisting.

"I accomplished a lot of work while I was in Paris, mother," he replied.

"Does that mean I'll soon be adding another one of your books to my private library?"

Mrs. Riggs turned around and reached toward a low bookshelf. She selected one of four leather-bound books from the shelf and handed it to Sofia.

"Here's the one I like best," she announced with pride. "Have you read it, Sofia?"

Astounded, Sofia stared at the book. She glanced from the title to the author's name, and handed the book back to Chandler's mother. "I don't understand. This book was written by Humphrey Stenberg."

As Chandler's face broke into a wide smile and Sofia's face turned crimson, Mrs. Riggs looked from one to the other in total confusion. "Chandler *is* Stenberg," she stated finally.

"When Chandler's first book was published, he didn't really know whether he had any talent or not, so to protect the family name, he chose to write under the name of one of our ancestors, long forgotten, by the way. That's his portrait over there. He was a colonel in the Queen's Regiment, as you can see from his attire."

But whereas the eyes in the portrait were cold and devoid of expression, Chandler's were happy and warm and full of mischief. The painting was enormous. It was a full-length portrait of a soldier in dress uniform, standing straight and tall, and his long face bearing a stern expression. The only characteristic that seemed to have been passed along to his descendants were his incredibly blue eyes.

"Humphrey Stenberg," said Mrs. Riggs, nodding respectfully at the impressive portrait, "might well have provided protection from above for my son. At any rate, Chandler's first book was such a resounding success that the publisher recommended he keep writing under the name of Stenberg." Amazed at what she had just heard, Sofia wasn't able to say a word.

Now she knew. She had read it in the works of Stenberg—Stenberg, who was really her Chandler, her handsome boxcar lover. *Chandler is Stenberg*, she kept repeating to herself, still unable to believe it. If someone had hit her on the head with a hammer, she couldn't have been more stunned. Well, why not? Why should she find that so surprising? He had all the required intellectual qualities. And hadn't she often asked herself where she had experienced a twist of mind before, or a certain charm, or the kind of duality that made his conversation so fascinating?

With some regret, she began to realize that the Chandler she loved was vanishing, the carefree, full of dreams Chandler, who had agreed to pose as her husband, the bank robbing Chandler, her Chandler. Suddenly, Sofia recalled the time she'd described to him how she thought Stenberg looked—brown hair, dark eyes. How he must have laughed to himself at her description. She felt humiliated, degraded, and angry at having been deceived. Her pride had received quite a blow.

Surprised by Sofia's silence, Mrs. Riggs asked if Chandler had never told her about his *nom de plume*. Sofia was livid with anger. When she finally answered, she looked directly at Chandler. "He had never told me anything—oh, Chandler! How could you have done such a thing to me? You saw the Stenberg books I had in my apartment. We even talked about them!"

Mrs. Riggs joined Sofia in her indignation. "What a dreadful thing to do! Chandler, what on earth were you thinking? Why would you keep such an important part of your life from Sofia?"

"Because I wanted to be sure she loved *Chandler Riggs*, not *Humphrey Stenberg*. Too many young women have fallen in love with me because I'm a well-known author, making a lot of money. That's why!"

"He kept me completely in the dark, Mrs. Riggs," said Sofia, no longer able to contain herself. "I didn't even know anything about you or your lovely home. I thought he was penniless and lazy. In fact, I was sure he didn't even want to do anything for a living. But I fell in love with him anyway."

"I was working very hard in that little room of yours, Sofia, though you knew nothing about it. I wrote page after page, by hand, if you please. I thought that if I used anything else, you would surely be suspicious!"

"That was monstrous of you!" exclaimed Mrs. Riggs. "The poor girl . . . I never did understand why you were renting that room when you had your own apartment in Paris, and a lovely one, at that!"

"An apartment in Paris?" repeated Sofia. *This was too*

much.

"On the Right Bank, my pet. Now don't panic! It's very useful for business purposes, as is the one I have in London. Besides, Bath isn't too pleasant during the winter, and mother likes to use my apartments when she travels."

Sofia just stared at him. "Just one more thing I didn't know," she said in a flat voice that belied her rising hysteria. "As matter of absolute fact, the only thing I ever really knew was that I didn't know anything!"

Mrs. Riggs was looking at her in astonishment. "And you still agreed to come here with him, my child?

"I love him, Mrs. Riggs," replied Sofia, her voice faint with desperation. "Stupid, wasn't it?"

"She loved me even when she thought I was a bank robber, Mother. Can you believe that? A bank robber?"

"Chandler, what are you saying?"

He didn't have time to answer.

The living room door opened a crack and the heads of two small black children appeared.

Two voices, each as timid as the other, spoke at the same time. "May we come in, Nanny?"

"Of course, my dears," answered Mrs. Riggs.

The door opened wide and the two young boys hurled themselves at Chandler, who caught them in his arms and squeezed them tight. They started an uninterrupted string of questions and answers. The boys called Chandler, "Uncle Chan," and seemed to adore him. They were both a little skinny, laughed easily and never stopped squirming all the time they were on their uncle's knee.

They spied the serving table and asked if they might have a roll.

"Didn't you have anything to eat this afternoon?" asked Mrs. Riggs.

"Yes, Nanny," the older one spoke up first, "but we always have room for more!"

Mrs. Riggs smiled and gave one to each of them. "If you can't eat it all, give what's left to one of the dogs," she said. "Now, take them outside and eat them. And please close the door when you go out."

They tore out of the room as fast as they had come in. Sofia, who had decided never to speak again, raised her eyebrows inquiringly. Another mystery, she thought. Chandler was ignoring her unspoken question, rising to his feet and straightening his tie.

Mrs. Riggs quickly spoke to clear up the matter. "Chandler brought Brian and Alan back from Biafra," she explained. "You remember the terrible war that took place there a few years ago? Practically the whole population was dying of hunger . . . the children looked like little skeletons. A few men risked their lives to fly in medication and food, hoping to save some of the children. Chandler knew one of the pilots and decided to go with him."

"But didn't the British support Nigeria?" Sofia asked.

"Oh, *support*." Mrs. Riggs sighed. "It's a meaningless word in terms of such a war. And victims are victims no matter what their nationality. Anyway, Chandler very much wanted to go, and he didn't care what anybody thought. I admit, it was probably a little foolhardy of him . . . but he has such a soft spot for people in distress."

"I'm no different than a lot of people," said Chandler. "I went there as a spectator and got caught up in what was a horrible situation. Those poor people! Children were abandoned, mothers were starving. I couldn't begin to describe the conditions those two boys were in when I found them. Their parents had been killed. They were left with only an aging grandfather to take care of them, and I promised him I would. What would you have done in my place? That poor old man died in my arms. How could I leave those children there?"

"You couldn't," said Sofia in a small voice.

Chapter Fifteen

Sofia remembered Chandler standing in her apartment, holding a book by Stenberg in his hand, reading the notes about the author. "Born in London . . . world traveler . . . visited Biafra and Vietnam." Oh, why couldn't he have told her that he was that man? Why couldn't he have told her about risking his own life to save those two children?

Their mother was already dead when Chandler had rescued the children. Now he treated them as his own. She couldn't help being touched, though this did little to diminish the anger she felt toward Chandler for having kept so much from her. But he had! Again, she could see him standing in front of her, saying indignantly, "What do you mean, I don't know anything about children? I have two of my own!" Then he had added, "Their mother? I never knew her." The whole thing was beginning to make sense. It had all been true.

"Naturally," continued Mrs. Riggs, "he wasn't able to bring them back immediately. First, they had to be treated in a hospital. When they arrived here, Brian and Alan were just skin and bones. They've finally become quite used to us and we are doing our best to see that they are raised properly. Later they can choose between Africa and Europe. It will be up to them to decide where they want to live. I don't think they will ever know how much they owe Chandler, but just the same, they adore him and always wait anxiously for him to come home."

Sofia listened, every trace of emotion drained from her.

Despite his good deeds, she simply couldn't forgive Chandler for not having trusted her. Apparently, Mrs. Riggs noticed Sofia's numbness, for she very tactfully offered to take her to her room.

From top to bottom, the house was bright and cheerful, and the fresh smell of furniture wax hung in the air. But although the place had a very relaxing atmosphere, Sofia had been upset, angered to the point that she was almost ready to explode. Chandler, Stenberg, she still couldn't believe it! Too many answers had been dropped in her lap all at once and she just couldn't cope.

Mrs. Riggs seemed to be aware of her distress, and, to distract her, stopped by the master bedroom to show her a picture of her husband. "You see," she said very calmly, "he was very much like the colonel downstairs. He had the same blue eyes, very remarkable they were, but fortunately my husband's expression was different."

A smile on her lips, she looked admiringly at the picture of the man she had loved, would probably always love. A portrait of only the head and shoulders, it showed a face that expressed noble intelligence mixed with kindness. It left no doubt that this had been a man of common sense and true loyalty.

So this was Chandler's father. Sofia recalled what Chandler had told her. This was surely the last straw! She had a sudden irrational urge to get as far away from this house as possible. Everything was the opposite of what she had been led to believe, from what she had imagined. She could feel her legs shaking, as she quietly followed Mrs. Riggs.

But Sofia wasn't in a mood to appreciate anything, no matter how lovely. Under different circumstances, she would have been delighted with her room. It was spacious and comfortable, beautifully furnished and with a décor bright enough to suit the taste of any young woman.

"I see that your luggage has been brought up," said Mrs. Riggs, glancing around the room. "If you need anything, please let me know. Don't be shy. I want you to feel at home here. Now, I'll let you get settled. Dinner will be served at seven."

"I'm very sorry, but I don't think I can eat a thing. If you don't mind, I'd rather just stay in my room . . . and go to bed early."

Mrs. Riggs was not easily fooled. "You're angry with my son, aren't you?"

"I would rather not see him tonight," confessed Sofia. Then she went on firmly, her head held high. "To tell you the truth, I would really like to go home. Do you think it would be possible for Jessy to drive me to the airport in the morning? I don't want to inconvenience you, but I don't have any other way of getting there."

"It won't inconvenience me, my dear, but I wish you'd think it over. I know my son loves you, and I know you love him."

"I did love Chandler, Mrs. Riggs, but I don't love Humphrey Stenberg," she said, a bitter edge to her voice. "I don't know a thing about Humphrey Stenberg. All I know is that Chandler Riggs has done nothing but make a fool of me. Do you think you'd be able to stand that?" Suddenly her eyes became moist, her nerve failed, and like a child, and she leaned against Mrs. Riggs and wept.

"I know how you must be feeling, my dear. Chandler was wrong not to have told you anything. But he has told you why he acted that way, and I'm sure he thought that once you were here and found out the truth, everything would be alright."

"He had no reason not to tell me the truth in the first place, Mrs. Riggs. Instead, he continually lied . . . really, it's more than I can bear! I did nothing but be good to him and nothing deserving of that treatment."

"Of course not. You're a lovely woman. But is the truth so awful, now that you know it?"

"Oh, no! Quite the contrary, in fact. Everything here is quite wonderful. But I had imagined something entirely different and had my mind all set to cope with it. If I had known about all this, I never would have allowed Chandler to stay in my apartment. I never would have treated him the way I did. The Chandler I loved is poor, has nothing. The Chandler I know needs someone like me to take care of him. Humphrey Stenberg doesn't need anyone."

"That's not true! Chandler Riggs, or Humphrey Stenberg . . . he needs you and loves you."

"He'll get over it—it's likely just a passing fancy, anyway. Games, you know?" she said what she feared. "Chandler's very good at them. I'm not presumptuous enough to imagine that Humphrey Stenberg could love me. I'm not the least bit ambitious, and I'm certainly not interested in his fortune. If he thought he would impress me with his childish revelations of wealth and position, he was seriously mistaken."

"Chandler certainly was mistaken," said Mrs. Riggs softly. "There's no doubt about that. Unfortunately, he too often arranges his life like he writes his novels. Things just seem to happen, one after another. But I'm convinced he is sincere in his love for you. You like the same things and you have the same education. And believe it or not, he shares your high moral principles. My dear, Chandler has written many charming things about you in his letters to me."

"And all the time, he was pulling the wool over my eyes," said Sofia angrily. "Playing his silly games, making fun of me, mocking my most sacred feelings." Then she added furiously, "I shall never forgive him for that—never!"

"Very well," said Mrs. Riggs, obviously downhearted. "In your shoes and at your age, I'd probably feel the same way, dear. Youth is so demanding these days. In any case, you must do what you think is best."

Realizing Mrs. Riggs was doing everything she could do to be kind, Sofia felt a little embarrassed at the way she had been speaking to her. "I must apologize," she said. "You have welcomed me with open arms, and I don't want to seem ungrateful. I will always remember your kindness. I can't marry Chandler now."

Mrs. Riggs smiled at her. "I won't argue, my dear. Right now, you're tired and confused. You must rest. Mrs. Banes will bring you a snack later, in case you feel hungry. And she'll bring your breakfast to you in the morning at eight. Usually we all have breakfast together, downstairs, but I can well understand that you will want to have yours in your room. At nine sharp, Jessy will be waiting to take you to the airport, that is, if you still wish to leave. In any case, all the rooms are equipped with house phones. Yours is right there on the table. If you should change your mind, it will be a simple matter for you to let us know." Then she added very kindly, "Would you mind very much if I hugged you, Sofia?"

"I would like that very much." They hugged each other for a long moment. It was with mixed emotions that Sofia watched Chandler's mother leave her room.

Alone in her room, Sofia waited for Mrs. Banes to bring her something to eat. The meal wasn't long in coming and looked delicious—chicken, salad, wine to drink, and cake for desert. "Thank you very much," she said.

Mrs. Banes nodded wordlessly, confirming what Sofia suspected—that because of her, the whole household was in turmoil. She didn't care. Too many things had happened to upset her. Angrily, she snapped the latch on the door and turned to glare at the phone on the table, daring it to ring. She hoped Chandler would call her, so she could hang up in his ear before he had a chance to say a word! But Chandler must have realized how seriously she had been offended, because the phone remained quiet. Nothing, in fact, disturbed her solitude.

The lovely home was wasted on her that night, and the sooner she left it, the better she'd feel. Her face felt hot. She tried to open the window and finally succeeded after some difficulty, because the shutters opened from the outside. She mumbled in aggravation. Her window overlooked a beautiful garden, which she would have found enchanting under different circumstances. And certainly her room was very pleasant. But Sofia found none of these things any more pleasing than if she had been in a hotel room overlooking the alley.

Little more than Chandler's toy. Her pride was sorely wounded. The realization that her nightmare had turned into a beautiful dream hadn't struck her. She felt no joy at learning the man she loved, with whom she had been prepared to spend the rest of her life even if he had been poor, was in fact wealthy, a famous author who was willing and more than able to make her life a fairy tale. She had conditioned herself to being kind and generous, even protective, and now the situation had been completely reversed.

She was no longer the one who would give. Instead, she would receive. In Paris, she meant something to the people who knew her. Here, she was a nobody. She no longer felt any passion for Chandler. In the past twenty-four hours, he had become something less than irresistible. He had caused her to be humiliated, and her anger eclipsed every other emotion.

"Oh, how I hate him!" she hissed through clenched teeth. "I hate you, Chandler Riggs!" she whispered.

It occurred to her that she was paying him a compliment by concerning herself with him at all. She would be better off just to go to bed. She took only the essentials from her suit-case, so she wouldn't have to spend time packing in the morning.

Even a hot bath failed to relax her. Although she wasn't hungry, she ate the piece of cake, then went to bed. Chandler never left her mind. Over and over, the first night shared in her apartment was the turning point for her. The way he caressed her, his kiss — warm, moist, and intoxicating. The way he touched her — it was no secret he knew how to please a woman in bed. She had never intended to fall in love with Chandler, it just happened. And now she hated herself for allowing it.

She lay waiting for Chandler to come knocking. Deep down she wanted him to stop her, come to her room and stop her. But that didn't happen.

Chapter Sixteen

The next morning, Sofia woke up, just as determined to leave as she had been the night before. Mrs. Banes brought her breakfast and she ate every morsel. All the time she was dressing, she kept looking at her watch. At nine, she went into the hallway to see if the car was waiting outside. It was.

Tears consuming her eyes, no matter how hard she tried to stop them, she grabbed her suitcase and hurried downstairs, hoping she wouldn't run into Chandler or his mother. But she needn't have worried. No one was there to see her off. Everyone was still sleeping. Despite all her good intentions, she felt her eyes stinging. Was she of so little importance to them? Had she been nothing more than a silly girl with whom they had their fun?

Even Jessy, who supposedly was so strict about protocol, wasn't going to open the car door or even help her with her suitcase. Sofia could hear voices in the kitchen, probably Mrs. Bane giving the children their breakfast. All the doors were closed. It appeared no one was going to make any effort to come out of the house to say goodbye. With a heavy heart, she reached the steps of the veranda and walked down to the doorway. Through her tears, she could vaguely see Jessy's silhouette behind the wheel. She recognized him by the cap and uniform. His face was turned the other way. He must have heard her coming, but he didn't move.

They're really letting me go, without a word. Annoyed with his behavior, she decided she wouldn't bother to wish him a good morning before telling him where she wanted to go. "To Bristol, Jessy. The airport." Sofia was crying openly by this point. She looked back at the house where she had been made to feel so welcome the previous day, but she couldn't see through her tears.

"Oh, well. Perhaps it was better this way," she said to no one. Still, she couldn't help resenting Jessy's attitude. Was he going to let her carry her own suitcase at the airport, too?

Why did she have the feeling that she had behaved like a rude, ill-mannered little girl ... especially when everyone but Chandler had been so kind Sofia dried her tears, angry at herself for giving in so sentimentally when she should have been using logic. She was leaving behind nothing but lies and compromise and moving back into her own world, where everything was clear and simple. So why did she feel so desperately unhappy?

She felt a stab of fear. While she let these thoughts ramble through her mind, she gazed at the passing scenery. Suddenly she realized they were not on the road they had used to come from the airport the day before. They were on a side road with absolutely no traffic.

"Jessy," she shouted. "Where are you going? I said I wanted to go to the airport."

To her great surprise, the car stopped, and the driver threw his cap onto the seat beside him, revealing dark hair that could belong to only one person. Sofia was horrified. "Chandler!" she cried in disbelief.

"Yes," he said, turning around, "'tis I." He looked at her and his eyes twinkled with mischief. "You've just been kidnapped! Want to call the police, darling?"

Sofia glared at him in silence and shock. She still couldn't find her tongue.

"Did you really think I'd let you go, my pet? Why don't you come up front and sit next to me, or should I come back there?"

"No thanks, to either! I want to go to the airport, now!" she shouted. "You can take me just as easily as Jessy."

"I will, later, if you insist, my sweet, lovable little pet. Although, I must say, now you're more like a dreadful grouch."

"It won't work, Chandler," she replied idly, "I'm going home." She started to cry, but bit back the tears for the moment. Sofia was almost beside herself with anger and wasn't thinking clearly.

"Alright," he said, "but before you leave, I want to know why you're going. No! Don't you dare get out of the car!"

He had spoken sharply, having noticed her movement toward the door. "Try to open that door, and I'll step on the gas. You'll just get yourself killed, and if you don't mind, I'd rather not have to explain away a dead body. Strange as it may seem, I would be very upset if anything happened to you. So just settle down a minute. You've wasted too much energy already."

"You are absolutely repulsive!" she cried. His words were the most shocking. Her mouth fell open and she stared at him is disgust. Unable to conceal her emotions, she bent her head to tears. "The only place I want to go is the airport!"

"I know, and I also know I'm madly in love with you. What can I do?" Chandler suggested quite happily, "Where shall we go for a quiet conversation? A lake, perhaps? The site of one of those old ruins? Some of those castles are quite picturesque. No comment? Very well then, I opt for the lake. Maybe the peaceful waters will calm you down. I certainly hope so. It's nothing fancy, just a small, man-made lake, but it is charming, and I know a place, close to the water's edge, where we won't be disturbed. Nobody will be around at this hour."

Chandler stopped the car close to the water, and he was right, there wasn't a soul in sight. He took a blanket from the car and spread it on the ground.

"Please, sit down. The ground slopes here and you should be quite comfortable. Be careful to sit on the blanket. It would be a shame to soil your new suit, especially since it looks so nice on you!"

"Chandler, stop the sweet talk!" snapped Sofia. "You shouldn't have gone to all this trouble just to whisper sweet nothings."

"You're quite right about that, my love." He sat down in front of her. "Now, I want to know why you're running away. Didn't you like the house? Oh, you did. Was it the dogs, then? Not that, either, eh? The children, perhaps? Wrong again. Then it must have been my mother."

"Your mother is a jewel and you know it!" cried Sofia, forgetting for a moment that she was furious with him. "She couldn't have been kinder to me, and I'm sure that everything she told me was the truth, too." Sofia was choking with rage.

"Thank you. My mother says I'm very much like her." Chandler smiled.

"Ridiculous! If that's what your mother says, she must still be thinking of you as you were when you were a little boy. You may have been charming as a child, Chandler, but now . . ."

" . . . and now, I'm abominable. Is that what you were going to say? Why?"

"Because of everything you've done, all the things you led me to believe. Do you think it's all right to walk into a girl's sleeper in the middle of the night, pretending to be tired, pretending not to have enough money for accommodations of your own?"

"I wasn't pretending! Everything I said was true. I told you I lost everything at the casino."

"Well, anyone who would gamble like that certainly can't

be very respectable," she said bitterly. Sofia looked at him, not knowing what to say. She had forgotten he was Stenberg. She was about to speak, when he continued.

"Agreed. But I wasn't playing for fun, or even to win. It was my first time in a casino. I had to find out what it was like, because in the novel I've been working on, the hero is a compulsive gambler. There are some things a person just can't invent. Sometimes I have to see things for myself before I can write about them with any kind of credibility.

"And I couldn't wait for the money from Paris. My French translator wanted to go over my work before sending it to the printer. If I had missed that meeting, it would have caused a delay in my novel being published. As it was, the printers were waiting for it."

Chandler's face was bright and smiling, his eyes sincere. "You know the rest. A silly pretext, I'll admit, to avoid getting into a hassle with the conductor. A pretext and a joke which would have been of little consequence, had your boss not been on that train. Later, you were the one who wanted me to stay, despite my warnings, and you asked me to be your make-believe husband, too."

"That's true, I admit. But why did you stay when you had an apartment of your own in Paris? A much more comfortable apartment than mine, I'm sure. I see. Then I was just a guinea pig for you?" she said, feeling offended.

"It was too tempting. Aside from the fact you're quite beautiful, the idea of such an experience fascinated me, considering that I would be staying with a usually very proper young lady.

"An adorable little guinea pig, dear — sometimes afraid, sometimes trusting, but always lovable. And I always had the greatest respect for you. Remember that night at your aunt's?" Chandler smiled. "Very well, we won't talk about it. Now, what else is making you so angry?"

Sofia blushed and replied dryly, "Let's forget that part of it, shall we? The night we talked about Stenberg, you never so much as hinted that you and he were the same person." The tender way he was looking at her was wearing her down, and without realizing it, her voice softened.

"I explained the reason for that to my mother yesterday, while you were there. If you'd known I was Stenberg, everything would have been very different between us. I wanted things to stay just as they were for a while. If you could only know how touched I was by the kindness you showed the poor devil you were putting up."

"Alright, Chandler." She sighed. "But I still don't fully understand. Being Stenberg, or even Chandler Riggs, for that matter, how could you stand that job wrapping parcels in a dreadful basement?"

"It wasn't all that bad, my love. As a writer, it was an opportunity to research a working situation that was completely new to me. Of course, I made it a little more fun," he added, with a smile. "If I ever must describe those working conditions in a book, I'll know how to get it across quite easily, because I've been there."

But at the same time, he had become something more, better balanced somehow, more serious and infinitely more capable. Sofia said nothing as she considered his intelligent face. She was discovering a new Chandler, and this one interested her. He was still her Chandler, with his charm, his smile, his teasing humor.

Curious, Sofia asked if he had experienced everything he had written about.

"Not everything. Although for the novel *Encounters*, I worked in a mine for ten days."

"Good Lord! You must have come out of there as black as the ace of spades!"

"You said it. After the last day of work, I took three baths, one after the other."

He was an artist, very much involved in his work. He was brilliant, full of imagination, honest and kind, and lived his life to the fullest. They looked at each other and both started to laugh. Chandler was no ordinary man. He could be a tease, sometimes impertinent, and often would do things that no one else would dream of.

Deciding to never doubt him again, she felt as though the warmth of the sunshine reflected from the surface of the lake was flowing into her heart.

"Well," said Chandler, "things seem to be going much better. But go on, darling. We have to get rid of every doubt."

Sofia would have preferred to have stayed silent and be taken into his arms. Nevertheless, she had to agree it would be best to have everything brought out in to the open. "You also told me your father was an alcoholic. That's not true, either."

"You must have misunderstood me, Sofia. I certainly never said my father was an alcoholic. You see, his doctor forbade him to drink. But, like so many other Englishmen, my father liked to join his friends for a drink at his club, and eventually it killed him. He was always very active. As a matter of fact, he was a highly-respected Member of Parliament. I'm sorry you were misled into thinking anything so dreary."

Sofia was sorry, too. Chandler, a writer, and his father, a politician! If she had known, she certainly would have behaved differently. But why had Chandler kept talking about how broke he was?

"Because I'm not wealthy, my dear. Whatever fortune there is belongs to my mother, and I'm not about to live off her. I live on the money from my books and a few investments I've made along the way. It's just that sometimes I get so involved in other things that I forget to go to the bank. If I am broke, it's usually only for a day. Now, does that make you feel better? Good! Is there anything else?"

"Yes, the policeman, who—"

Chandler's hearty laugh interrupted her. "Ah, yes! You still think he was there to arrest me. Actually, he was there to help me solve some problems concerning espionage that I was planning to use in a future novel."

"Then why did you run away? Why did you leave France in such a hurry?" asked Sofia, who, by this time, was beginning to feel foolish.

"I didn't *run away*, my dear. That trip was planned. My seat was reserved for that Saturday afternoon and I didn't want to miss my plane. By the way, I'd spent that Thursday you were so concerned about meeting with the producers of a film they're making of one of my books, *Boxcar Lover*. Come to think of it, I believe that's one you've read."

"Yes," said Sofia. "It's quite delightful, very . . ."

She rephrased it, knowing full well she might be asking for trouble. Suddenly, Sofia remembered the car, and the guy in the car, the other woman . . . she knew now it had been nothing more than coincidence—yet she still felt jealous. She realized he still hadn't really answered her question why he rushed off to Milan.

"What about the woman you took with you to Milan?"

Chandler smiled. "I didn't take her with me. I went to Milan to meet her. She never leaves Italy. I'm surprised you didn't recognize her. That was Michelle Leann. She's going to play the female lead in the film. Fascinating woman, indeed, but incredibly difficult! God forbid I should ever fall in love with anyone like her. I had to see her because she was demanding some radical changes in the script. They were impossible, of course, but it took a while to convince her . . ."
Chandler laughed and looked at Sofia. "You're certainly be-

ing very thorough in your examination, dear."

There was still one more thing that had been puzzling her. "Tell me, Chandler. Why did we walk out of the restaurant that night? Didn't you want your friends to meet me?" Sofia's eyes widened as she looked at him. She knew he was telling the truth.

"It was the other way around," he replied. "They were people in the film business, who knew me by the name of Stenberg, and I wanted to be just plain Chandler for a while longer. You loved me for me, my sweet one, and you'll never know how much that means to me."

With a smile, Chandler continued. "Maybe I was being selfish, but you must admit even though I may have confused you about a lot of things, I never really lied to you. I simply kept a few things from you, and your imagination did the rest. Instead of coming closer to me, you kept going the opposite way. And if I let you do it, it was only to teach you a lesson. Taking a stranger into your home and making him your husband could have been very dangerous."

"You're quite right about that!" Sofia agreed, although she wasn't angry any more, nor did she feel humiliated. She finally had learned the facts and now could see everything in true perspective. Filled with happiness, Sofia listened, as Chandler went on.

"Believe me, it was never my intention to mislead you or make fun of you. I'm sorry if you thought it was. And if I hurt you, I can only hope you'll forgive me." Chandler knelt in front of her and took her hand. His face expressed such love, such genuine concern, that Sofia's heart melted.

"Oh, Chandler, I'm so sorry, too," she cried from the bottom of her heart. "I shouldn't have been so suspicious. I had no reason to get angry to the point of hating you and wanting to leave. Any other woman wouldn't have acted so irrationally. If only I'd known."

"But you aren't any other woman, my darling, and that's why I love you. I've loved you for a long time, and it killed me to have treated you in such a way. Do you remember the day you came home late, and I accused you of being with another man? I've been angry with myself ever since for behaving so badly. I seldom lose my temper, but I was so unhappy, so jealous . . .

"And even before that I loved you, Sofia. Remember the day we went to church together? Very important, my love. I knew I was falling in love with you and I asked God to help you feel the same way about me.

"Oh, my dear," she whispered, so deeply touched, she was close to tears.

There was no need for her to say any more. Chandler had taken her into his arms. Being considerate and tactful, Chandler didn't drive immediately to his mother's house. They needed time to themselves to fully realize their new understanding and enjoy each other's company.

He spoke of the receptions they would have to give and the trips they would have to take, either for newspaper articles, or for research for his books. They stopped for lunch in a small village near the lake and walked in the countryside, making plans. Chandler talked about his family, his work, his publishers, and the people in the film world with whom he associated.

She was a good secretary, Sofia thought, happy to have had the kind of business experience that would allow her to continue to be active. *I can take his notes and keep up with his ideas. An active life, full of diversity, no more empty existence. And, of course, there'd be children.*

That the man she loved was both Chandler Riggs and Humphrey Stenberg no longer concerned her. Since Chandler considered her good enough to be the wife of a famous author, she would see to it that he would never have reason to regret his choice. Already, she could feel new forces stirring within her, and her enthusiasm, once she really belonged to Chandler, would only grow. She would discover her real self—something she had always hoped would happen.

"Dear Humphrey," she whispered suddenly.

It was the sign of her final acceptance.

The End

About the Author

Riley Michaels lives on a farm in the foothills of the Blue Ridge Mountains with her horses and pets. Married 31 years with one son, one daughter, and two wonderful grandkids. She has a degree in Animal Science with a minor in Animal Husbandry, and six certifications in her field of study.

Riley is a world-renowned wood burning artist whose work has been shown in seven countries, appeared on four TV shows, exhibited in galleries and museums, and won awards. She is also a retired National Champion figure skater. Her hobbies are her horses and her pets . . . and more recently her writing.